# Training A Hockey Star

Van Cole

Published by Van Cole, 2022.

TRAINING A HOCKEY STAR

**First edition. December 18, 2022.**

Copyright © 2022 Van Cole.

ISBN: 979-8223335788

Written by Van Cole.

# Table of Contents

# Training a Hockey Star
# Gay First Time Romance

**By: Van Cole**

# Foreword

My Nightmare Client Became My Lover, a Hockey Star Treated my Heart like a Puck

I thought my dreams had come true when Rudy Marsh came back home and decided that I, Josh, was going to train him during the off season. All I wanted was to be a fitness trainer and now I had one of the hottest stars in the business. He would be the catalyst for my success, all I had to do was treat him well.

But God he didn't make it easy. From the first moment we met he acted like he was my enemy, torturing me, tormenting me, pushing me to my limits because he knew I was desperate.

And then it happened. He made me do something I never thought would happen.

He pushed me too far and I realized I liked it. We went from enemies to lovers in a hot romance.

# Training a Hockey Star

# Chapter One

Josh

I was sitting on my couch with a beer in my hand watching a clip of Rudy play. He's one of the all time greats, and I feel proud that he comes from my little corner of the world. I guess the rest of us do as well. It wouldn't surprise me if a statue gets erected of him by the time his career is over. It's not like our small town is famous for anything else. Rudy is an inspiration to us all, and it's easy to see why. Watching him on the ice is like watching a master artist at work. The ice is his canvas, the hockey stick his paintbrush, except by the end of the game he's cloaked in blood and sweat rather than paint. I watch as he surges past an opponent, their hockey stick is flailing in the air as they try to trip him up, and fail. Then he swivels, before striking the puck. It's like he's pulled off a magic trick. One moment the puck is by his stick, the next it's in the goal and the keeper is standing there, as stunned as the rest of us. Rudy turns away and lifts his stick in the air triumphantly. He pulls his helmet off and I can see the pure joy on his face. It's infectious and I can't stop smiling.

That's the effect he has on people.

That's the effect he has on the whole town.

He's a goddamn hero, and he's going to be my client.

I take another swig of my beer to calm my nerves, and I wipe clammy moisture off my palms. Skin peels off my lips as I gnaw at them and I wonder if I'm actually going to be able to pull this off. I'd only contacted him on the off chance that he might want some training on the off season. If I managed to get a good review from him then my fledgling business could take flight. I was never going to be as successful as Rudy, and there certainly wasn't going to be a statue of me near the town hall, but I could at least make a name for myself and become a success, which is more than most people could hope for in this place.

Rudy is going to be my first client and I almost can't believe that he's going to entrust his fitness to me. I keep thinking that it's some strange dream, that I'm going to wake up and find out this is all make believe. Look at him, the crowd is cheering him, pinpricks of light flash behind him as they try to capture his image in a photograph. I just know that he's the key. If I can get him as a regular client then who knows who else I'll be able to get? But he's the crown jewel, he's the one I really want.

The only thing that's surprising to me is that, as he wheels away after scoring, none of his teammates skate beside him. It's as though he's alone on the ice, as if he has the entire world to himself. I know what loneliness is like, although I don't imagine he's alone off the ice. A man like him must always have someone around. There is something ethereal about him, something that makes him larger than life, something hypnotic. It took a while before I realized how long I had been staring at him, but that was the mark of a great man. They held the world in their hands, and nothing could rip it from them.

*

It was the first day of our training session and I paced about the gym nervously. I'd rented out a small space. It was humble, but it would do, considering I only had one client. I'd been studying furiously, so much so that I'd barely slept the past few nights. Nerves were churning in the pit of my stomach and I kept shifting my gaze between the clock and the door, for Rudy was late.

Maybe I had been too optimistic to think that Rudy would actually show up. I was a trainer with no reputation, just starting out, and he was a hockey star. Of course he could have done better than me. I looked around at my humble beginnings and let out a dry chuckle. Sometimes I wondered if I should have done what Mom said and thrown away this dream because it was never going to put food on my table. But I didn't want to end up like everyone else here.

I wanted to be like Rudy.

Then it happened.

The door opened and he walked in. I didn't realize until a few moments later that I had been holding my breath. The air seemed to shimmer around him, and that was how I knew I was in the presence of greatness. He seemed larger than life on the TV screen, but in person the effect was magnified. He looked like a giant, and my lips parted in awe.

He looked around at the gym and nodded, then walked up to me, holding out his hand.

"You're Josh I guess?" he said in his pleasant drawl. I took his hand. The grip was firm, his smile magnetic, and his eyes seemed to drill right into the depths of me. This was the difference between people like him and people like me. He made an impression on people.

"Yes, that's right. It's a great honor to meet you, and I'm glad that you're here. I look forward to working with you," I said, trying to remain professional, but it was difficult to not let my fawning admiration seep through.

"Yeah, well, I thought I'd better keep myself tuned up during the off season. I wouldn't want to lose that edge," he said, and dumped his exercise bag by his feet.

"Of course. I've researched a lot of diets and I've put together a few nutrition plans based on what you want to accomplish on the off season. I don't know if you want to put on some extra muscle or if you just want to maintain things for the moment," I said, trying to keep my voice calm. Nerves were bubbling inside me and I didn't want to appear unprofessional, like I was just some fan who caught a lucky break, which as it happens is what I did feel like.

Rudy scoffed. "Don't you think I'm in good enough shape already?" he asked, flexing his arm under his tight t-shirt. It was impossible to not admire his figure, purely from an aesthetic perspective of course. The angles of his body were illuminated in such a way that they flowed from one to the other. It was as though he had been sculpted by a master craftsman, every imperfection chipped away until what was left was this pure form.

"Sure, sure," I said, feeling sheepish. What right did I have to tell this successful athlete how to look after his body.

"Look, I'm not going to lie, all I really need is for someone to help me stretch and things so I keep limber. The season is intense and I don't want my off season to be all serious. I don't get the chance to come home often so I'm planning to enjoy myself, and that involves drinking copious amounts of beer and relaxing a little."

I tilted my head and summoned up my courage. "Are you... are you sure that that's a good idea? I mean, you don't want to lose your touch for the season."

As soon as the words slipped out of my mouth I regretted saying them. His head snapped around to glare at me, and his eyes were like two shards of ice, cutting and chilled.

"Are you going to tell me how to manage my body? Don't you think I've picked a few things up considering I've played hockey... oh... let's see," he started to count on his fingers before he yelled, "all my life!" He marched towards me and I got a sense of what other players must have felt when they collided on the ice. "Let's get one thing straight," the words flew like bullets from his mouth. "I'm not here because I'm paying for the best. I'm here because the club needs me to have someone watching over my fitness so they can have peace of mind. I'm not doing this for me, I'm doing this for them, and the sad thing is that this rinky-dink town doesn't have anyone of the caliber I need. So congratulations, you've got the job. If you play your cards right then this is going to be the easiest job you've ever had because all I need is a few sessions a week and then a report sent to the club. Other than that, I plan to enjoy myself while I'm home. And you get to say that you have me as a client. Frankly I would have thought you'd be jumping for joy. Do you know how much of a big deal I am?"

"Y-yes," I stammered, averting my gaze because I was afraid of the thunder in his eyes.

He prodded me in the chest. "Well then, I hope that you know you can stuff your nutrition plans because I've had enough of that. I'm not going to do anything I don't want to do, and if you try and push me, then I can bury you just as much as I can make you. Do you understand?"

I swallowed a lump in my throat. Suddenly my dream had turned into a nightmare and what else could I do but go along with him? He was Rudy "fucking" Marsh, and I was just a nobody. I had to do what he said.

The worst, most humiliating thing was at the end of the session. He'd dismissed me and I was sitting on a chair, waiting for time to crawl by so that I could get out of there. I never thought holding a training session with Rudy Marsh would end up making me feel like crap. I watched him go through the motions, going far gentler than I would have been. He barely warmed up before he told me that he was ready to go, but before he did he had something he finally wanted me to do. At first I was just glad to actually do my job. I started to rise, assuming that he wanted my help to stretch or something, but I had barely lifted my butt out of the seat when he pulled it towards him and placed his foot on top of it, pulling his shorts so far up his groin I was one inch short of seeing his stick and two pucks. I guess it was his way of asserting his dominance.

"I'm feeling a bit tight Josh. Do you mind giving it a bit of a squeeze before I go?" Rudy asked. There was a smug, sneering look in his eyes. I glared at him and gritted my teeth. I knew he wasn't doing it because he truly needed my help. He just wanted me on my knees, to remind me that he was in charge here. If I had been a stronger man then maybe I could have stood up to him. Maybe I would have told him that he was a cruel bastard and nobody should have to put up with this treatment. But the fact was that he had me over a barrel. I knew it and, more importantly, he knew it. If I walked out now then he would tell everyone that I failed him, and nobody would ever hire me again.

So I sank to the floor, bowing my head to hide my shame. Frankly, I didn't even want to look at him. I grabbed some lotion from my bag and squeezed it into my palm. The gel was cool against my skin as I rubbed it in. Then I placed my hands upon his thigh, feeling the strong muscles. They were so taut, so powerful. As someone who had spent a lot of time studying the human body, it was impossible to not be impressed with the state of his. His fitness was impeccable and even though he was a jerk, I couldn't deny that his body was one of the best I had seen. I pressed my fingers around his thigh, feeling the supple flesh underneath my finger tips. There were dark hairs that swept along his tanned skin like wild grass in the desert. I couldn't feel any knots in the muscles, so I was doubly sure he was only doing this to make me feel like crap. Still, I wasn't going to let him get away with it. I rubbed him as hard and as good as I could. If nothing else I hoped that it might prove to him that I was actually great at my job. I wrapped my hands around his thighs and squeezed, feeling the heat of his body emanate around my hands.

"Go lower. My calf is starting to feel tight too," he said. I grimaced, but said nothing as I did as he asked. I figured my best bet was to just grit my teeth and get on with it. If I could just put up with his bullish behavior then at the end of it I would at least be in a better position, and I'd be more likely to get some clients. I brought my hands down behind his knee, feeling the soft flesh of his calf muscle. I looked at the pale veins that ran underneath the skin, each one of them were rivers carrying life throughout his body. My fingers sunk into his flesh. My gaze flicked up and glanced at the rest of him. I couldn't help but wonder what he looked like under all those clothes, how sculpted and pristine his torso must have been. I never usually preoccupied myself with so many thoughts about the male form, but when in the presence of someone like Rudy I couldn't help but wonder what the apex of human conditioning could be, and how close he came to it. As he stood there with his foot on the chair, looking up at the ceiling, he looked like he was posing for a statue to be made of him. I wished I had been stronger. I wished I had been able to assert myself. It was something of professional pride that I should be concerned with the way he treated his body. The last thing I wanted was for him to grow lax and lose the fine conditioning his body was in. It certainly wouldn't reflect well on me, and it wouldn't do him any favors either.

As I massaged his flesh I dreaded it becoming soft and flabby. It deserved to be hard. His body was a temple and it deserved to be worshiped by fans. Even though Rudy had inspired nothing but hatred for him from me, I was still in awe of his flesh. It was impossible not to be. I imagined that anyone in my position would have been the same. They would be mesmerized by the way his flesh glistened after it had been coated in oil, by the way the firm elasticity stretched under the weight of fingertips pressing against it, and they would have been transfixed by the feeling of it. It was so warm. I found myself being entranced by it, as though his flesh was a vast desert of unblemished smooth sand that was waiting for someone to mark it with footprints. It was so easy to become lost in a man like him.

I shook the thoughts from my head, telling myself that there was a point where professional interest went too far. I quelled the fluttering feelings in my stomach and told myself that I was being foolish. I didn't need to be in thrall to this man, no matter what kind of shape he was in. I was just here to do a job, and I was going to do it about as well as I damned well could.

# Chapter Two

Rudy

Being back at home was a strange sensation. It had been a long time since I had returned. I liked coming back here, you know, I mean, it's not exactly a chore to come back to a place where you're worshiped, but there's something about being a big fish in a small pond that I just don't like. These people, they put all their hopes and dreams onto me, like I'm some kind of talisman for their success. It's almost like they don't have to try in their own lives because they can look at me and think 'yeah, he's made it, that's cool, I can just live off his glory'. I never wanted that responsibility. I never asked for it either, and yet I find myself carrying the burden anyway.

But what do I know? I guess if people want to treat me like a king then I'll let them. There's no harm in it after all, and it's not as though I don't deserve it after everything I've done on the ice. Countless player of the season awards, records broken for goals scored, scoring streaks, winning streaks, you name it I've done it, and everyone here loves it.

Usually I hate the off season, but this time I'm looking forward to it. My body could use the break. It's not that I'm old. It's still a few years until I turn thirty, but the last few seasons have been tough. My body has been through the wringer and all the seasons have taken their toll. The last thing I need is to train too hard over the off season. I didn't want to train at all, except that I was forced to. Despite being a big shot hockey player there's always someone else calling the shots. Unless you're an owner you don't get to do shit, even though I'm the one making them millions. I'm glad for the break. Something happened that left a bad taste in my mouth and I need some time to sort my head out.

Have you ever wondered where your life is heading? For someone like me it's always been a straight line to the future. Even when I was young I knew where I was going to end up. I was too good as a hockey player to ever be anything else. I've never believed in destiny or any of that shit, but some things are written in the stars I guess. But I know that it's not going to last forever. I can already feel my body creaking. I've got a few seasons left in me, but how many at the top? I've seen too many other legends fade away because they don't know when to quit.

For the first time in my life I'm staring at a blank slate. When my time on the ice is over what is there for me? I have to try and make it last as long as possible. God I miss the days when I knew exactly what I was doing, when life was simple. Over the years it's gotten more and more complicated, and more people like to butt their noses in. At least back here I'm away from all of that shit. The last thing I need is for someone to tell me what to do here as well, which is why I don't have much hope in this trainer.

You'd have thought people would understand that I've been doing this long enough that I know my body, but no, they need forms for the insurance and all that crap. Well the joke's on them. I chose the cheapest, freshest asshole, who won't dare to stand up to me. I'm going to be training the way I want to train and I'll have fun doing so. I might even see how far I can push him. I loved the look on his face when I told him how things were going to be. He looked like a deer caught in the headlights. He stammered and spluttered and looked as though the rug had been pulled from under him. This was only the beginning of his troubles because it's a long time until I'm on the ice again, and I have a lot of frustration to get out of me.

Of course, there's another stop I have to make before I go to the apartment I've rented.

I pulled up outside the old familiar house. I shake my head, wondering why Mom and Dad never took me up on the offer to buy them a new one. The door is hanging off the porch and the paintwork is flecked. I could have given them a nice mansion, but all they wanted was to stay here. I paid off all the bills for them, of course. It was the least I could do for all the hours they spent driving me to and from practice and letting me hone my skills, even when they would have preferred me to hunker down and focus on college.

I walked in and stopped in my tracks. It wasn't only my parents there. They'd asked Annette too.

There she was, my high school sweetheart, still with the raven hair and the soft lips, and the lingering look that always suggested more.

"Hey Annette, I wasn't expecting you here," I said.

Annette smiled, as though she was aware of the trap that had been laid. "Yeah, it's funny the way that works," she flashed a smile to me, the kind that she always used to flash when we shared a private joke. "Your Mom invited me round and I couldn't miss the opportunity to see you again. It's been a while."

"Yeah, well, you know how it is," I said, glaring at Mom and Dad. Mom giggled to herself as though she was some kind of master puppeteer, while Dad got up from his chair and shook my hand. Mom eventually came over and hugged me.

"It's good to see you son," Dad said. The hair on his head had thinned, and was something that I had to guard against.

"I'm not sure why you're not staying here though. We have your old bedroom made up. You don't want to be spending so much time on your own. You're at home, this is a time when you want to be with family," Mom said.

I tried to be as diplomatic as I could because I didn't want to hurt her feelings, but sometimes I got the feeling they still thought I was a teenager. I guess maybe because they don't get to see me in my day to day life.

"Mom, you know that I'm not here just for a vacation. I still have training to do. We don't get to just take time off. I'll be exercising and reviewing matches and all sorts of things."

"That's fine, we'd still love to have you back," she said, and as she smiled at me sweetly I felt like a damned monster. But Annette was there for the save.

"If he's as messy as he was back at school then you definitely don't want him around," she laughed. Mom laughed too and the tension was defused. I smiled my thanks at Annette and that was the end of Mom trying to get me to stay with them, for the evening anyway.

We had dinner and spoke about the usual things. Dad had kept up with all my games, of course, and we talked through the season with him. I have to admit I was curious about what was happening with Annette though, and I only got to talk to her once dinner was over. We went out on the porch with a couple of beers.

"Welcome home," she said, clinking her beer bottle against mine.

"So, what's new with you?" I asked. Mom had always given me brief updates on Annette's life over the years, but it was good to hear it directly from the source.

"Well, you know, I got married and then divorced, so that's something," she said, wearing a wry smile. I'd heard the tale from Mom, the tragic tale of Annette and Bryan. I couldn't believe it when I heard it from Mom, and I still can't believe it now.

"Yeah, I'm sorry to hear that."

"Don't be, it was a mistake from the beginning. I just wish I'd realized it at the time."

"I don't mean to be disrespectful or anything, but what the hell was it with Bryan? He was the last person I thought you'd end up with."

Annette laughed and swept a hand through her hair, pushing a handful of cascading dark hair away from her face. It was the same mannerism she'd had when we were together. Suddenly the past was rushing up towards me like a torrent of water. I was back being a teenager, with all the raging hormones and the uncertainty and the feeling that one kiss from her was going to blow my mind.

"Yeah, well, things changed. You know. Life wasn't easy for me after high school. I lost my Dad and college... well... college just went down the drain. I was searching for something and he was there for me. He was there at the right time and I think I confused companionship with love. I was too afraid to be alone. For a time I was able to delude myself into thinking that something would grow and we could be happy, but I'm just not that kind of person. I have to be in love with the person I'm with, and I was never going to be able to fall in love with Bryan. So things ended."

"I'm guessing he wasn't happy about that."

"No, he wasn't. Thankfully he's not the angry kind of guy. He's the weepy kind. I feel bad you know. But life never works out the way you think it will. I never thought I'd be married and divorced before I turned thirty. I guess it's different for you though. Your life has turned out exactly as you planned."

I shrugged. It wasn't possible to deny it, although my life was far from perfect. I understood what she meant about that longing for companionship. As my career was starting to wind down I was beginning to realize how empty my life was when you took away everything regarding hockey.

"It has, yeah, but it's not exactly everything it's cracked up to be. To honest, at the moment I'm starting to feel like I'm back at high school again, right around the time when it was ending. I know my career isn't going to last forever and I have to start thinking about what I'm going to do afterwards. I had the same feeling in high school, except then I knew that I was going to be a hockey player."

"Is the great Rudy Marsh going to have to live like the rest of us?" Annette teased.

I shot her a look. "I'm sure I'll figure something out," I said. "I'm sorry Mom dragged you into this by the way."

"It's okay. She means well. Besides, it was good to see an old friend. Reminds of a different time, a time when things were simpler."

I thought she was going to say better, but perhaps simpler was a more appropriate term. We were just kids when I had left her the last time. She had been in tears. I pursued fortune and fame in the big city, and she was left here, left behind. Sometimes I wondered what my life would have been like had I stayed with her. Maybe she would still be married. Maybe we'd have kids. It was the American idyll, but that had never sat right with me. As much as I loved Annette for everything she meant to me, even now I wasn't able to imagine a life with her.

I guess I just wasn't the kind of guy to settle down.

We spoke for a little while longer and then she left her beer on the porch. She said it was nice to see me again and kissed me on the cheek. As her lips brushed against my skin I let myself wonder what it would be like to experience a real human connection again, but as tempting as it was to relive my childhood I wasn't about to revisit the past. I couldn't hurt Annette again, and I knew that's exactly what would happen. She had been through too much. At least I could count on her as a friend though.

I said goodbye to Mom and Dad, and they made me promise to stop by as soon as I could. I left them and returned to my quiet, empty apartment. I hadn't bothered to bring many personal things with me, but it struck me how desolate the place looked. It dawned on me that, when I was finished with hockey, this is what my life would be like. It's not like anyone would want to bother with me when I'm not on the ice.

I'm just going to be pointless.

I hate it.

# Chapter Three

Josh

It's time for my second session with Rudy. I got up early because I couldn't sleep. My legs were jittering all night with nerves and my mind was reeling. I kept imagining myself telling him what to do, but I knew it was just a fantasy. He had made it clear in no uncertain terms that he was in control and I had to do what he said. I hated it, and I kept telling myself that the only way to deal with bullies was to stand up to them. It was easier said than done though. It always had been.

I'd never been the athletic type. At school I was a runt, the smallest in my class, and everyone knew I was the guy to pick on if they were having a bad day. There was one guy in particular who made my life a living hell. Alfie Dean, his name was, a big brute of a kid that looked like a giant. His head was as thick as a wooden post and he was the kind of guy you could see was going to be trouble from a young age. He was a kid with no future, and it was just a matter of time before he was behind bars. I wish he had been locked up sooner, but when you're kids there isn't any sympathy for crimes against each other. You're just told to get on with it and the adults act like nothing went wrong. Every day Alfie came to me and punched me in the gut. He threw my bag in mud, pushed me down, stole my lunch. It became a grim routine and every time it happened I told myself that tomorrow would be the day when I stood up to him. Tomorrow would be the day when I embraced my courage and became a man.

That day never came.

Instead I became better at hiding, but there was no hiding from Rudy. It was deflating to know that Rudy was a bully. I had hoped for better from the small town hero.

I was waiting in the gym for him, breathing deeply to try and calm my nerves. I glanced at the clock and my watch to make sure they were both running at the correct time. They were. It was Rudy who was late. Again. I paced back and forth, and checked my phone to see if he had sent me a message. He hadn't. I scrolled through my contacts and thought about ringing him, but my hand hovered over the name, hesitant with nerves. I knew what kind of rebuke I would get if I called him, but then I told myself that I was supposed to be a professional. Part of being a trainer, especially a successful one, was dealing with the egos of these athletes. If I couldn't handle Rudy then how was I ever going to be able to handle anyone else?

Just when I was about to call the door burst open and he came in, acting nonchalant as though nothing was amiss.

"Morning," I said through gritted teeth. He flashed me a smile and dumped his bag on the floor. He began to stretch. "You know, the least you could do is turn up on time. We should at least get a full session in."

Rudy was standing with his legs stretched apart and his body angled, with his left arm arching over his head. He glared at me and resumed a normal standing position. "Are you really going to do this now? I can't be late, because I decide when I train. Sometimes I might not show up at all. I wouldn't think you'd mind, it means you get paid for nothing. This is going to be the easiest job you ever had."

"I don't want an easy job. I want to do my job. I want to train you. At least let me lead you in stretches."

"I've been stretching myself since I was a kid. I think I know what I'm doing. Just relax Josh, come on, fuck, I bet you were the guy in class who always asked for more homework when you were done."

"I like to keep busy, what of it?"

Rudy laughed and shook his head as he resumed stretching. His shirt was tight and accentuated his muscular figure. Given my profession I had an admiration for a healthy physique and Rudy's was perhaps the best I had ever seen. Every inch of him was honed to be a powerful machine on the ice. His muscles were taut, his shoulders broad, every angle was sculpted to perfection. It pained me to know that he wasn't invested in maintaining it to the best of his ability.

"Man, you need to learn how to relax."

"Why? Let me guess, you were the guy who always did his homework at the latest possible time?" I shot back, hoping that something I said would work its way through the cool exterior and actually annoy him like he was annoying me. He brushed everything off with his uncaring air and that laugh that drilled into my mind.

"Actually I never bothered with my homework. Didn't see the point in it."

I looked at him aghast.

"You didn't see the point in homework?"

"Of course not. I knew from when I was a kid that I was going to be a hockey player. Homework was just a waste of time when I could have been training."

"Oh, so you actually did training then," I muttered, rolling my eyes.

Rudy seemed to find this amusing. "Yes, I did training then. I always worked hard to be the best. It didn't just happen overnight. But the point of all that hard work is that I get to reap the rewards now and I get to take it a little easier than usual. You should learn to enjoy the good times while you can. I bet you didn't enjoy school either. I bet you were always putting pressure on yourself to succeed. Don't you realize it's all a con? What does it matter whether you did well at school or not? Do you really think it's helped you in life?"

"It helped me learn how to study."

"What, so you can get a qualification in fitness? It's hardly the most privileged position."

I could feel the anger rising within me. Heat bristled under my skin and it was turning crimson. In that moment I hated him more than any other person I had ever met, even more than Alfie Dean. There was no need to be this cruel. I hated myself for being so weak, but tears began to form in my eyes and my hands balled into fists.

"Look, you can come in here and insult me and do whatever you like. You can tell me that this is a waste of time. But I've worked hard to get to where I am and I've put a lot of work into this business. All I want is to be a personal trainer. I don't have to stand here and take this abuse from you," I said, and turned to walk to the end of the room.

I heard Rudy sigh. He ran after me and grabbed my shoulder.

"Okay, look, that might have been out of line. You have to understand that I'm from a hockey team. We rib each other all the time. I guess I forget that the outside world isn't like that. I get that you're starting out and maybe I'm not the ideal client, but it doesn't change my point that you just need to chill out. Isn't it everyone's dream to get paid for doing nothing? Just go and sit down and relax, it seems like you could use it."

He took his hand away from my shoulder. I couldn't decide whether he was actually being nice or if this was just a way to get me to calm down. Like with Alfie Dean I backed down and nodded. I slunk back to my position, leaning against the wall as Rudy continued with his workout.

"So what are you doing today then?" I asked dryly when I had worked up the courage to speak to him again.

"I'm just going to do some circuits, work on my cardio, nothing too intense," he said.

I held my tongue as he burst into a sprint up and down the gym, turning sharply, stopping abruptly. His muscles were like pistons and I couldn't help but push my dislike for him away and admire him. He was in great shape, and it was no wonder that he was at the top of his game. Still, as I watched him I noticed his cheeks puff slightly and I wondered if he was getting to the point where the workload was beginning to challenge him. His hockey game was intense. No man could do it forever. Was the great Rudy Marsh coming to an end?

When he stopped his face was drenched in sweat and his skin was a shade of crimson. His chest heaved, and his shirt was soaked, so much so that it highlighted his muscles even more dramatically. He might as well have been naked. He grabbed some water from his bag and arched his neck back, gulping down the water dramatically. Then he poured some over his face to wash the sweat away. It left his hair dripping.

"Is that all you're doing?" I asked. He looked at me.

"For today, yeah. I told you I was going to take it easy."

"Aren't you afraid your body is going to get used to taking it easy? What happens when you have to get intense again when the season starts?"

"I'll be fine. I know my body. I trust my body. I can handle this. I've been doing this for season after season. Do you really think I'm going to let myself go back to the team out of shape?"

I shrugged. "I don't know, you are the guy who never bothered to do your homework after all."

His mouth twitched into a smile, not that there was anything good natured about it.

"Come on, I've got something to show you," he said, and headed out of the gym. I glanced up at the clock. The session ran about an hour short and I shook my head. I didn't know how to get him to take this seriously. He was in control when I was the one supposed to be telling him what to do, but he wasn't prepared to listen to me at all.

We walked outside to his car, which was sitting in the parking lot. He opened the trunk and pulled out a bag. He peeled off his shirt and tossed it in the bag. I glanced at the flecks of sweat trickling down his torso. There was a layer of dark hair rippling across his chest that was the epitome of manliness. It was as though he was a statue someone had sculpted. There was a sharp intake of breath as I let my gaze linger upon him. Despite despising everything about his personality I couldn't help but be in awe of his body. It was a testament to human strength that a body could be forged into such a weapon. I had seen him plastered over magazines before, but seeing him in the flesh was something else. A strange temptation flashed through my mind, a temptation to touch him. His body was like a flickering flame that danced and writhed and made you want to touch it even though you knew you would get burned.

I was shaken from my reverie as he pulled the bag towards me. When I peered into it I could see that it was filled with clothes.

"Do me a favor and take these to the dry cleaners. Bill me for however much it costs, and add a little something for yourself if you like as well. It shouldn't take too long to do, I only have the essentials in there," he said.

I stared at the bag and then I stared at him. This was not in my job description.

"You want me to do your laundry?" I asked, trying to understand if he was actually being serious.

"That's why I brought it here," he replied, as though it was my question that was strange rather than his request.

"Rudy, I'm here to train you, not to run errands for you."

Sometimes with bullies their moods changed, as though a switch had been flicked. It was like this with Rudy. There was a dark look in his eyes. He glared at me, angry at me for daring to challenge him. He stepped closer to me. When I breathed in I smelled the sweaty aroma of him, the deep athletic musk that simmered on his flesh.

"I told you that you're going to do what I want you to do. You want to make my life easier, right? You don't want me to report that you've been difficult. Remember that my assessment of your abilities is going to make or break you. If you want to be successful then you're going to have to get on with what I ask you to do. Besides, you said you always liked to ask for more work, so here's your chance to go on and be a teacher's pet. Go and be a good boy and do as you're told," he said, mocking me with his eyes and his voice. I was back in school all over again, still the runt, still too weak and too cowardly to fight back. A lump formed in my throat. I wished I had enough courage to summon something to say to him. I glared at him and I wondered if he could sense the frustration pouring out of my eyes, but if he did he didn't say anything about it.

I turned away from him, hating myself as I did so, and grabbed his bag of laundry. Before I could say anything else to him he had already turned to answer a phone call. I stared daggers at him, but that was the extent of my assault.

I drove away and gripped the wheel so tightly that my knuckles turned white. I berated myself. When I glanced in the rear view mirror I looked at myself with disgust. I always assumed that when I grew older I would be a better man, a stronger man. I always thought I would be able to stand up for myself when someone challenged me, but at the first test I had failed. The world was filled with bullies and I was the one they picked on. I stared at his laundry, wishing I had the courage to go and throw it in a ditch or maybe even sell it to avid fans. I wondered how much a sweaty jock strap would fetch on eBay, but then of course he would be angry with me. He'd tell the world that I was a crap personal trainer and that would be my career left dead in the water before it had even begun.

The only way I could cope with this was to tell myself that I was doing it for the greater good. If this is what it took for me to have the career I wanted then I was just going to have to put up with it for a few months. It was a due I had to pay, like actors in Hollywood having to put up with asshole directors and shitty scripts just to get their name out there. If I had to do a little laundry to get Rudy's seal of approval then so be it. Once I was an established name then I would be able to set the terms to my clients and I would be able to lay down the rules they had to follow.

That's what I told myself anyway. Deep down I wasn't sure I believed it. I had a feeling that no matter who my clients were I would always be at their mercy. I would always be the one being told what to do. It was almost as if it was in my nature, and I hated it.

# Chapter Four

Rudy

I felt bad for Josh. Not bad enough to stop treating him like this, but bad enough to pity him. After all, it wasn't his fault that he had been burdened with me when I was in this state of mind, but he really wasn't doing himself any favors with trying to get me to follow a regime. What did he think I had been doing for the past decade or so?

It didn't help that I was a little worried. In the sprints I'd gotten out of breath sooner than I'd imagined, and he'd managed to get to the core of my worry. I was concerned that I wouldn't be able to get back to my best in time, and if that happened were people going to start talking about the decline of Rudy Marsh? I was able to push the thought aside. How could they dare to even suggest that Rudy Marsh was declining?

But then I got the phone call that changed everything.

Josh had just gone off like a good boy to do my laundry. I figured I might as well make good use of the time he was being paid for. Then Shane called, my devoted, devout, determined agent.

"Hey Rudy, how's home life treating you?" he asked. His voice was tinny and strained over the phone. I paced around the parking lot, hoping that I could find some area where he came through clearly.

"Yeah, it's all good. It's nice to have a break. I wasn't expecting to hear from you. What's up?"

"Oh, nothing really. I just wanted to check in. How's the personal trainer working out for you?"

"I've only had a couple of sessions so far, but it's promising," I replied. It wasn't exactly the truth, but it wasn't exactly a lie either.

"You know the guys aren't too happy about you going rogue and using someone who has no reputation. They're a little worried."

I rolled my eyes. "I know they're worried. They made that perfectly clear to me before I left, but I told them what my thinking was and they're just going to have to deal with it. I want someone who has some new ideas, some fresh thinking. This guy is good, I'm telling you, real good. I got myself a bargain. In a few years people are going to be begging to be trained by him."

"Alright," Shane said, although I could tell he wasn't convinced. "I just hope you're right. You need to come back in top shape when the season starts again."

"Of course I will. When have I ever not?"

"Look, I know you've been having thoughts, you know, about the future."

"What are you talking about?" I asked. Part of what made Shane such a good agent is that he often knew what I wanted before I knew I wanted it. But then it led to moments like this and I was annoyed that someone could have a window into my mind.

"We both know it's been coming Rudy. People can't go on forever. There comes a time when you have to start thinking about what comes next. I know you still have a few good years left in you, but it's never too early to start to plan."

"Shane, you're acting like I need to retire now."

"Well, you never know what might happen. One bad injury-"

"People have been saying that to me my whole career. Nothing has changed now. What's going on? You've never sounded this concerned before." Shane paused before he answered and I stopped pacing. As much as he knew what I was like, I knew his quirks as well. Whenever he had bad news to deliver he always took his time about it, and I started to feel that uncomfortable, unsettling feeling churning in my stomach.

"Look, it's not really anything right now, but I've been hearing some rumors and some rumblings that you might want to be aware of."

"What kind of rumors?" I asked.

He sighed again. Dammit. Sometimes I wish he would just get on with things.

"Like I said, it's nothing really too major, it's just that I heard through the grapevine that we're not the only ones planning for, you know, the end."

"What are you talking about? Who else is planning for it?"

"Management," he said. I should have known before I asked the question really. My heart sank and the world felt as though it was beginning to crumble.

"Who are they thinking of signing?"

"Like I said Rudy, it's really just rumors at the moment. There's nothing concrete about it and I haven't spoken to them directly myself. I just wanted you to be aware that it's on their minds."

When management had something on their minds it was always a bad idea. Sure, they had the good of the team as their focus, but that meant the players were expendable. They weren't ruled by sentiment and they weren't about to give anyone a chance that was undeserved. If they thought my time had come, then my time had come, and there wasn't a damn thing anyone else could do about it.

"Who are they thinking about signing Shane?"

"Jesus Navarro," he said after another pause. The words were like knives in my heart. Jesus was a hotshot kid who was tearing up the league. He'd made no secret of the fact that he wanted to be the best there ever was, and that meant he was going after my records. He'd already broken my youngest player record by a matter of days.

"I guess he's the kind of guy that management would go for. He's got fire in his belly."

"Yeah, just like you did when you came on the scene. I'm sure there's nothing substantial in it and they're certainly not looking to push you out. They just have to keep their options open, but I wanted you to be aware of these rumors in case anyone asks you about it, okay?"

"Sure thing Shane, thanks for keeping me in the loop."

"You've got it. At least this trainer is putting you through your paces. I'm sure you'll come back and you'll show them that nobody can touch you. This Jesus Navarro might be someone one day, but he sure as shit ain't ever going to be Rudy Marsh."

"Damn straight," I said as Shane ended the call. I must have sounded calmer than I felt. I almost smashed the cell phone on the ground. I stormed back to my car and slammed the door behind me, and then I hit the steering wheel. How the fuck could they do this to me? I knew how management worked. They were insidious little serpents who didn't care about the game of hockey at all, at least not in the romantic sense. All they cared about was moving people about like little pawns in the hope they could maximize their revenue. They had squeezed every drop out of me and now they were looking for the next guy to drain. Well, my day wasn't done yet and I wasn't going to let them replace me before I was ready to leave. I was only going to go on my own terms, not when they were ready to shuffle me out the door, and I wasn't going to let some kid take my place either.

I snarled as I revved the engine and drove back to my apartment where I paced around. I was like a wild animal. I actually started to wonder if I had made a mistake in coming home and leaving the team. Memories were short. People were always quick to forget. I knew I shouldn't have done it, but I went online and looked at videos of this Jesus Navarro. I hadn't played against him yet, but I could see similarities between me and him. If they signed him then it would be a battle between young and old, and there was only ever one winner there. If nothing else time would grant victory to the young, and then instead of Rudy Marsh's name being chanted in the crowd it would be Jesus Navarro.

Christ it was depressing trying to prepare to go out with dignity. I wondered how many players felt the same way I do now when I came on the scene. Back then I thought it was going to last forever. I thought I was going to be immortal.

I guess I was wrong.

*

I was seething in the dark when there was a knock at my door. I wondered who could be coming by. At first I thought it might be Annette, and to be honest I would have welcomed her company at the present moment. It wouldn't have been the worst thing in the world to have an old friend to listen to my troubles. I opened the door, only to find Josh standing there. I was a little taken aback.

"Here's your laundry," he said, thrusting the bag into my arms. I took it and breathed in the fresh smell of linen. I dumped it on the floor. He was already turning away. I could sense his annoyance, but I wasn't ready to be left alone to stew in my own dismay.

"Josh," I called out. He stopped and turned his head halfway towards me. I grabbed my keys and wallet. "Let's go for a drink." I never gave him the opportunity to decline. Maybe he thought that I was rewarding him for a job well done. Really I just didn't want to be alone.

We walked outside and headed towards a nearby bar. It was a quiet night, although the bar had a healthy number of people. When I arrived and they noticed me they all went crazy. I smiled, embracing the love of my fans. There was no better feeling than being worshiped and adored. It wasn't quite the same feeling of standing in a stadium with the crowd bursting with admiration, a cacophony of noise swimming around me, but it was still better than being in an empty apartment dwelling on the ever extending shadows of the future.

Chants grew around us.

Rudy! Rudy! RuuuuuuuDY!

I waved and nodded and accepted my free drinks. I nodded to a table. Josh seemed overawed by the reception. As soon as we sat down people hovered nearby. They glanced my way as though I was an exhibit at the zoo. There was always a strange attitude where people were afraid to butt in on my life and bother me, yet they never fully kept their distance. I could sense their whispers and their excitement. It made me laugh. A few people were brave enough to come up and ask me to sign their shirts or their napkins or anything they could get their hands on. I obliged them and thanked them for their comments. Some of them said they used to watch me play when I was a kid. That was going back years now, but it was a testament to how much the memory of fans lasted for. It wasn't like management, who wanted to shuffle players off as soon as their form started to drop or as soon as the age started to be a concern. No, players became legends in the minds of fans, and the glory days were relived over and over again. It did provide me with some comfort to know that I was going to be eternal in the thoughts of these people, and that long after I was gone there would still be someone, somewhere, saying 'Rudy Marsh, yeah, he was a damn fine hockey player'.

I spent about twenty minutes or so chatting with the fans as they came up to me. Even the shy ones grew brave enough to approach when they saw that I wasn't going to snap at anyone. Eventually I got around to everyone who wanted some attention. Excitement bubbled around as they all admired their little piece of memorabilia and enjoyed the sensation of meeting a celebrity.

"Is it like this wherever you go?" Josh asked.

We were sitting at a round table. We each had a bottle of beer. A bowl of pretzels was between us, which I shoved into my mouth. Josh was wearing a light shirt that was open at the collar. He was in good shape, as I would expect a fitness trainer to be. He had a very clean look though, as though he had never really dipped his toes in the grime of life. Part of me wondered what he was like behind closed doors. He was a few years younger than me, but the difference seemed more apparent because he was so naïve and cherubic. I almost felt bad for teasing him.

"Pretty much. It depends where I go. In the city there are a hell of a lot of fans, so yeah, whenever I step out of the door I get attention. Back here I'm the home town hero. I'm just flattered that people still remember me. Eventually there's going to come a point where I come back and people aren't going to recognize me."

"I don't think that's going to happen. You're the most famous guy ever to come out of this place. Without you this place doesn't really have much going for it," Josh said.

"That's very kind of you to say," I admitted, and raised my bottle to him.

"I just don't know how you do it. Doesn't it just take you ages to get anywhere if you're always bothered by people?"

"Yeah, sure, but I don't see it as being bothered. People spend their time and money cheering me on and buying shirts with my name on them. They hang posters of me up on their walls, and they spend their evenings watching me play a game of hockey. The least I can do is give them some of my time in return. I get that a lot of people don't want to be bothered. I've known a lot of guys who absolutely hate it and just want to be left alone, but at the end of the day these people are just excited to meet someone who brings them joy. I think I'd be cruel if I begrudged them that."

Josh nodded and I took another gulp of my beer. I also knew I had to enjoy this while it lasted, not that I was going to admit that to Josh.

"I guess that's good of you," he said. "I don't know if I'd be the same."

"I'm sure you would. You don't seem like you have a mean bone in your body."

"No, I guess not," he looked away, and I got the sense that he was disappointed.

"You're going to have to get one if you want to make it in this world. It's hell out there, it's a war, and if you don't fight for yourself then you're never going to make anything of yourself. People are always going to take and take and take, and you don't want to get in the habit of giving everything you have, because you're just going to be drained dry. You have to stand up for yourself."

"Is that what you did?"

"Hell yeah! When I went from the minor leagues to the majors nobody wanted to give me the time of day. Sure, I had the talent and I had the numbers, but I was still a rookie in their eyes. There had been plenty of other great players who couldn't handle the pressure of the big leagues and washed out. I had to make sure I wasn't going to be one of them."

"So how did you handle it then?"

I leaned forward and smirked, enjoying one of my fondest memories. "The first game I played, I looked for the biggest guy I could. As soon as I went on the ice I charged at him and showed people I wasn't going to mess around. When he crashed to the ice, I announced myself and people knew that I was going to hold my own. It's a team game, but you have to look out for yourself. I played my best and that means the team is better, but you can be damned sure that over the years people have tried to drag me down and take my place."

"And none of them have succeeded."

"Not yet," I said, leaning back and draining my beer. A dark thought entered my mind and I slammed the bottle down on the table, shouting for another to be brought over. Jesus Navarro might be angling for my career, but he wasn't going to ruin my night.

# Chapter Five

Josh

I couldn't believe that I was actually sitting at a table with Rudy in a bar and he was being nice to me! When I dropped his laundry back I told myself that I was going to be angry with him. I couldn't bring myself to shout at him though, not with his threats looming over me, so I went to storm away. But then he'd invited me out. Maybe finally he was starting to see me as a real human, and potentially even a friend. I was amazed at how good he was with the crowd. It was like he was a completely different person, as though a different part of him came alive when he was with his fans. He was generous with his time and easygoing. When they were nervous he put them at ease. When they wanted to joke with him he laughed and teased them back. He seemed like a real man of the people, and I almost couldn't believe this was the same man who was giving me so much trouble.

I was caught in the spotlight with him, reflecting the radiant glow of this star. People noticed me, when usually their gaze would pass over me without ever taking note of who I was. Up until this point I was a nobody but now, suddenly, I was the man sharing a drink with Rudy Marsh. I noticed people whispering as they stared and they must have all been wondering who I was. I kind of liked the mystery, and I sat up a little straighter as they looked at me with envy.

The beers flowed easily as the barman was eager to give Rudy anything he wanted. As his trainer I was concerned as they started racking up, but I wasn't sure if I should say anything. The night was going well and I didn't want to ruin it, but I also had a job to do. I would have been letting down my client if I didn't say anything.

I leaned in and kept my voice low so that nobody could overhear us. I certainly didn't want people to think I was babysitting Rudy.

"Hey, Rudy, I'm not saying this to judge or anything, it's purely from a fitness standpoint, but don't you think you've had enough to drink yet?"

Darkness flickered in his eyes and there was the Rudy I knew. He licked his lips slowly. "I'll have enough to drink when I say I've had enough to drink." His words slurred and as if to punctuate his point he downed the rest of the drink he was currently holding and called for another one.

"I'm just a little worried. You know what this can do to your body," I said.

"I don't give a damn. It's my body and I can do with it what I like. Do you think I'm not going to make it back when the season starts?"

"I never said that. I'm just concerned, and I wouldn't be doing my job if I didn't say anything. But go ahead, I guess I shouldn't be concerned when you clearly aren't." I sat back and folded my arms across my chest.

"You've got a real sharp tongue on you. How dare you speak to me like that. You think you're someone just because you have a qualification? That doesn't count for shit in the world. The only way you're going to get work is if I recommend you. No-one else is going to hire a nobody," he said.

I don't know if it was because I had some liquid courage surging through my body or if the more time I spent with him the braver I was becoming, but I was ready to fire back. A wide grin spread across my face as I looked at my bottle of beer.

"You know Rudy, I've been thinking about the situation we've got here and I've started to realize that you don't have as much power as you think. Sure, you might be able to give me a bad review and prevent people from hiring me, but it's not like management is going to like hearing about you drinking yourself into a stupor, are they? I'm sure it won't do your public image any good to hear about how your personal trainer has decried you for being lazy, and for not giving the proper care to your body."

My words lashed out like a whip, and I could see him visibly shake with tension. It felt good to actually strike back at him after he had been treating me like crap. I liked that I could affect him as much as he affected me. He snarled, and I got the sense that he wanted to hit me. Maybe if we hadn't been in a bar he would have, but for a man like him image was everything. He couldn't risk something showing up on the Internet of a barroom brawl. He drained the last dregs of his bottle and then rose from the table.

"Follow me," he growled. We left the warm comfort of the bar. The night was chilly. I pulled my jacket more tightly around me, although Rudy didn't seem affected by the cold at all. He strode away towards the cab rank, but before we reached them he turned and thrust his finger in my face. He pushed my back against a wall. There were barely inches between him and me. His breath swirled into a fine mist that rose between us, curling in the air. I could smell the alcohol pouring out of him. His eyes were bloodshot.

"Don't you ever talk to me like that again or threaten me. I'm Rudy Marsh. You think anyone is going to believe you over me? You don't have any power here. I can make you do anything I want," he said, pushing his face even closer to mine, so close that our lips were almost touching. My entire body was rigid. My blood was like ice. There was a moment when everything went quiet and I thought the impossible might happen. It was just an errant thought that crashed through my mind, flashing like lightning. It was stupid because it was so far from what I wanted. It was crazy how much the mind played tricks on me when alcohol was involved. For a moment I almost believed he was going to kiss me. For a moment I almost believed I wanted it.

"I'll see you in training tomorrow," he said, his warm breath tickling my chin. Then he spun away and swaggered towards the cabs, his footsteps erratic. It was only at that point that I realized I had been holding my breath. I let it out in one long exhalation and then turned away, retreating to my car.

*

The night had been one of surprises. I wasn't sure how many people could say they had shared a beer with Rudy Marsh, and I wasn't yet ready to boast about it. I shrugged off the effect I'd experienced with the few beers I had drunk and returned home. Being in a small town meant the roads weren't busy at all, so I could take it nice and slow and not worry about getting into an accident.

When I got home I splashed water in my face and climbed into bed. I couldn't stop thinking about Rudy's face being so close to mine, and when I thought about Rudy I couldn't help but think of that moment when I had massaged his leg. Even now, days later, I could still sense the soft feeling of his skin. The more I thought about him the more his body seemed to unfold in front of me, and the more I tried to resist, the harder he lingered in my mind.

I was glad when sleep finally came over me giving me a respite from all these confusing feelings. I was sure that as soon as the new dawn rose I would be able to sort out my thoughts and return to normal, and I was beginning to hope that Rudy's stay in our small town would be as short lived as possible. At least then I could get on with my life and not have to worry about what was going to happen after Rudy left.

*

I was surprised to find Rudy at the gym the following morning before I arrived. He was already working up a sweat. His grey t-shirt clung to his skin and dark shadows highlighted the angles of his muscles. My throat went dry as I saw him and remembered how close we had been the previous night. I gulped and walked up to him.

"Getting an early start?" I asked, trying to sound happy. Despite the way the night had ended I hoped that sharing an evening with him had cooled his temper somewhat. I was mistaken.

"If you don't have anything worthwhile to say then don't say anything at all," he said, grunting through his breaths. His gaze was focused on the space ahead of him. The treadmill rolled underneath him, a steady stream of black against which his feet rose and fell. His cheeks were flushed red.

I frowned, annoyed at the way he greeted me. I took a breath to compose myself and reminded myself that I was a professional and I could cope with a difficult client. It wasn't as though he was going to be my last.

"You should have waited for me. I should have fitted you with a monitor so I could track your heart rate."

"Then it's your own fault for being late."

"I'm not late, I'm on time."

"In this game if you're not early you're late. Better you learn that lesson now than later," he said. I rolled my eyes and crossed my arms. I watched and waited for him to be done, concerned at the way he was pushing himself.

"You know there's such a thing as being too focused. You're going too hard Rudy. I think it's best if you take a break."

"I know my body," he shot back.

"Rudy, you don't want to do anything too intense right now. You haven't built up to it."

"Christ, first you want me to go hard and then you want me to go easy. Make up your mind."

As if to make a point he slammed his hand on the treadmill and jumped off. He glared at me, wiped his face with a towel, and then walked to another piece of equipment.

"Aren't you even going to cool down?"

"I'll cool down later," he said, turning to face me, "look Josh, I'm going to be honest with you. I'm not training today to get fit. I'm training because I'm angry. I just want to get a few things off my chest."

"Why are you angry?" I asked.

Rudy straddled the bench and then began straining against the weights. I waited for him to speak, but no words were forthcoming. When I got into personal training, part of it was to connect with people on a personal level, get involved with their lives, and help them improve their conditioning. I wanted to build relationships with my clients, not to treat them as strangers.

"You know you can tell me what's on your mind. I thought we had a chance to get to know each other last night," I said, unable to hide the aggrieved tone from my voice.

"You were just a convenient body to hang out with. It's not like I would have called you up to hang out if you hadn't shown up. I wouldn't go thinking too highly of yourself Josh. We're not friends. We're barely acquaintances. You're just here to help me check a box on a form. You wouldn't be able to understand what's going on anyway. It's not as though you're a part of the industry."

Ah, so it was something about his job. The way he was training it must have been something that really got under his skin. His muscles were bulging so hard that I could see all the rippling veins underneath his skin. His forearms were like tree trunks, and once again I was swept away in the magnificence of the man.

He sat up and swung his legs off the bench, flexing his arm, wincing a little in pain.

"Have you overdone it?" I asked smugly.

He glared at me. "It's just a little pinch. I'll get over it. I think I've had enough of this for the day anyway."

"You know we need to go over your nutrition plan and the regime for the rest of the week," I said forlornly, knowing that he wasn't going to care about any of this. He slaked his thirst from a bottle of water and shook his head.

"I thought we talked about this Josh."

"I thought we did too." I lowered my voice and stepped closer to him. "I thought I made it clear that I'm not afraid to tell people what you've been up to. Do you really want your reputation to take a hit?"

It was the one ace I had to play, but it didn't have as much effect as it had the previous night. Rudy looked confident as he glanced at me.

"You know, I admire you Josh. Despite everything I've thrown at you, you haven't given up. But the thing is you still have a small town mentality. I don't blame you. I had the same thing when I was growing up here. It took me a while to get used to the way the world really works too, but the thing is that you don't understand yet. Do you realize how many athletes get caught doing dumb shit that the club covers up? Nobody is going to care if I've had a few drinks. Nobody is going to care if I get into a fight. It'll all wash away because people don't like their heroes to become villains. You can crow all you want, but it's not going to change a thing. Have fun coming up with the nutrition plan. Email it to me later and I'll make sure to forward it along to the club. I'm sure they'll like to know I'm looking after myself."

I was left dumbfounded as Rudy walked away. I thought I had finally found a way to turn the tables on him, but in the end we were back where we started, except I had even less hope than before.

# Chapter Six

Rudy

I left the gym with a sigh of relief. For a moment there I wasn't sure Josh was going to believe my bluff. The truth is that management would care if I was shown to be getting drunk in a bar, especially when Jesus Navarro was on their radar. All it needed was one slip from me and my career would be spiraling down the toilet. Maybe I should treat Josh a little better. I hate anyone having control over me, but his opinion does matter. At the same time though it's just so easy to dump on him. He's like a puppy. I fear for him, making it in this industry. It doesn't seem like he has what it takes. You need to be ruthless. You need to be able to stand up for yourself, and he just doesn't have it.

He tried last night. God, what a night that was. I hadn't intended to get that drunk, but I forgot how good it was to have a beer. It helped me see things in a clearer light as well. What I really needed was to talk to someone who knew me. Once I'd gone and cleaned myself up after training I changed and headed out to see Annette. Seeing her again meant a lot. I hadn't realized how much I'd missed her. I got annoyed at Mom, but sometimes she pulled a little magic out of the bag. Maybe it was time for me to start thinking about the future, after all, Annette was still single and maybe that meant something. There had been a gap in her life, and soon enough there would be a gap in mine. I was going to have to find something to fill up the hole left by hockey.

Annette greeted me with her usual sweet smile, the smile that had been such a big part of my life when I was younger. I saw it so many times, but not when we parted. I hadn't thought of that night for a long time, mostly because it was too painful for me. It had been a hard night. I had been torn between staying here for Annette and leaving to pursue my dreams. Deep down I knew what I needed to do, and I thank God that she hadn't asked me to stay because I don't know if I could have left her had she begged me. She was in tears, I had been stoic, and we both left this life we could have had. Maybe I would have been happier with her, maybe not, but maybe we could get a second chance. People got those in life, right? It happened sometimes.

"I heard you were out last night," Annette said as she welcomed me into her home. It was the type of home I would have expected from her; humble and cozy with no flashy ornaments at all.

"I forgot how quickly word travels around here," I replied, a little annoyed that every movement I made was going to be reported on like it was some grand gesture. I guess that out here they're starved for news.

"You'd better believe it. You made a lot of people happy. They like meeting their hero. People have been wondering for a while if you're ever going to return to your roots."

"Yeah, well, I guess everyone has to come home at some point."

Annette smiled. She curled her hands around a mug of coffee. I relaxed into her soft couch. "I'm glad you still think of this place as home."

"Of course I do. This is where I was born, where I was raised. I wouldn't be the man I am today if I hadn't grown up here. This place will always mean a lot to me... as will the people." I looked at her directly and let my gaze linger. She caught my eyes for a moment, but then they darted away.

"You'll be going again soon though," Annette said.

"I will, for a while. But I won't be gone forever."

"You won't?"

I shook my head. "Things change. People move on. I have to start thinking about the next phase of my career. I'm not blind to the fact that I'm getting older."

"You and me both," she joked.

I wasn't sure it was a laughing matter.

"Are you sure you should have done that last night though?" she asked, concern creeping into her voice. I guess that was the problem with coming to her. She knew me, including all of my demons.

"I'm fine," I said tersely.

"It's just that when you were younger you almost-"

"I know what I almost did. I'm fine. I'm in control."

"Okay. I was just worried. If you're under pressure maybe you should speak to someone."

"I don't need to speak to anyone. And I'm not under pressure," I lied.

She huffed and stared at me. I hated the way she stared, like she was somehow gazing into the depths of my soul and I couldn't do anything about it.

"Rudy, you came here for a reason. Talk to me. There's something on your mind, I just know it. Even though we haven't seen each other for years I know you too well to ignore when you're struggling with something."

I threw my hands up and huffed. I suppose I shouldn't have been too upset with her considering there was a reason why I came to her in the first place.

"Fine, look, the truth is I got some bad news. I heard from my agent that the team are looking at some kid to replace me."

"Isn't that the nature of sports? There's always someone waiting in the wings to come and be the next big thing," she said.

"I know, but the fact that it's happening to me, now... it's just not something I thought would happen so soon. I thought I had a few more years at least. I'm starting to feel like an old dog whose owners suddenly bring home a lively, happy puppy. I just know that soon enough I'm going to be sent to the farm."

"I'm sure it's not as bad as all that," Annette said. She was trying to be gentle, but she didn't know the half of it.

"Management are ruthless. If they think I'm done then I'm done, and there's no two ways about it. I'll get a grand send off, lots of tributes will pour in, and then it won't be long before they're all cheering for

Navarro. It's the same thing that happened with me. I've just been blind to the fact that I've been so close to the end."

"I'm sure it's not all that bad. You've still got a lot of good years left in you."

"All it takes is one bad injury or one slump for him to get a chance, and if he takes it then I'm done. That's how I got into the game."

"So what are you going to do about it? It's not like you to accept defeat. I can't imagine you walking away from the rink with your head hanging."

"I'm not going to quit. I'm just... assessing my options for the future."

"And what might they be?"

I looked around at this home, wondering if I was going to end up here. "I don't know. I guess that's part of the reason why I came back. I'm not sure I'd want to stay in the city if I'm not playing hockey. It might be nice to come back here and make my life come full circle. There are always loose ends to tie up, mistakes that are meant to be corrected."

Annette rose abruptly. She turned her back to me and went to the window, where she looked out to her garden. I leaned forward on the couch.

"Some mistakes you can't make up for," she said.

"Really? I thought everyone was able to get a second chance at things."

"Not at everything," she said, and turned her head to look at me through the veil of her hair. "I think I know what you're getting at Rudy, and I think it's for the best that you don't think about this any longer. What happened, happened and it's best to leave it in the past," she said.

I furrowed my brow and leapt to my feet. In a few strides I had crossed the room towards her. I smelled the coffee and her perfume, the warm, comforting smells that should have felt like home to me.

"Annette," I said, trying to sound as gentle as possible, "you know I'm sorry for the way I left things. But look, it's hardly like life has worked out for you here, has it? Maybe this was always meant to happen. Maybe our story hasn't finished yet. We've just been waiting for the next chapter."

Annette shook her head slightly and gnawed on her lower lip before she spoke. "I appreciate that you've come here Rudy and it's nice to see you again, but you can't expect to pick up where we left off. Do you think I've been sitting here pining after you?"

"No, not at all. I just thought that since you're alone and I'll be alone maybe it makes sense to be together."

"Things don't have to happen just because they make sense," she said. "I can't do that to myself Rudy. Do you realize how much you hurt me when you left? I can't just forget about that."

"But that's in the past Annette. People change. Besides, you know I had to leave."

"No, you didn't," Annette said with more emotion in her voice. She closed her eyes, blinking back tears. "You chose to leave. You could have chosen me. I know you think that you had to leave because you wanted to be a hockey player and that's fine. The fact is that you still chose that life over one with me. I don't blame you and I'm not angry with you, but I can't ignore that it happened either. You will always be the man who chose hockey over me. You've always put yourself first Rudy. It's who you are. It's what has made you so successful, but it also means that you can't be completely happy in every area of your life either. I can't just ignore that hurt and that heartbreak, and I'm never going to know if there will be something else that will take you away from me. I'm never going to be your priority. I made my peace with that a long time ago, and I'm not going to change my mind now."

Her words stunned me. I had no idea she held this much anguish inside her. I knew leaving had hurt her, but she had always told me that she understood and that she didn't hold a grudge against me.

"Annette, it wouldn't be like that this time. If you had told me that you felt like this maybe it would have been different."

"No, it wouldn't have," her voice trembled with emotion. "You were always going to choose hockey Rudy. If I were younger then I might well give you another chance, but I don't want to put myself through that again. I'm not even sure if you really want to be with me anyway. This is all some way for you to deal with the fact that your career is coming to a close. The only two things in life you've ever been are a hockey player and my boyfriend. You can't just flip between the two. I'm worth more than being a backup option, okay? Look, I'm happy to be your friend and I'm happy to hang out with you and offer advice, and if you do end up moving back here then that will be great too. I still like you. I'm just not going to put my heart on the line when I know there's a good chance it will be broken again. I haven't exactly had the best of luck with men, so I want to make sure that I get the next one right."

I suppose I couldn't disagree with her logic, but I didn't have to like it. I knew there wasn't anything I could say to change her mind so I stormed out of there, filled with anger.

*

I was sitting in my apartment when there was a knock at the door. I swallowed the remaining golden liquor, feeling it slide down my throat, and then welcomed Josh. He sighed when he looked at me. Sure, I wasn't in a great state, with a slack t-shirt and alcohol stained breath, but I didn't care.

"You look a mess," he said.

"I've had a bad day. Pour me a drink." I dropped the glass on the counter next to the bottle and sauntered back to the couch. I heard him sigh, but he poured the drink anyway. He was a good kid really. He came towards me and handed me the drink.

"You know what I'm going to say, don't you?"

"Sure," I rolled my eyes and took the drink down my throat. "I know this isn't optimal conditioning, but I don't give a fuck. I think I've earned a few relaxed days now and then."

"I'm not sure you can afford to have any relaxed days, not if Jesus Navarro is going to sign."

As soon as he mentioned the name of that bastard my head snapped around and I glared at him.

"What the fuck do you know about Jesus Navarro?" I barked.

"I know that there's a rumor he's going to sign, and I know that he plays in the same position as you. There are already some articles being written about whether this is going to spell the end of King Rudy Marsh. It might be that you're already becoming a forgotten man."

I snarled and clasped my hands together. "They're a bunch of hacks who don't know anything. There have been people calling for the end of my career since the beginning. I'm not going to listen to them. They can all go to hell. So can Jesus Navarro. If he thinks he can waltz into my team and take my place then he's got another think coming. I'll take him down just like I've taken all the other pretenders to the throne down. Where are they now? I'm the only one left standing," I said. The words flowed out of me in a hot torrent.

"You were younger then. This kid is good from what I've seen."

"And what do you know?"

Josh stepped forward into my eye line. "I know a damn sight more than you give me credit for," he barked back. Recently he had been showing me his edge. I liked it. "Despite what you think of me I do know my shit. That's how I got this gig in the first place, remember? I hardly think you'd have hired me if I didn't know anything. I know what makes a good athlete, and he has it in spades. Pace, power, strength, he's got it all. He's got what you had. And you're going to lose it quicker than you might like to think. Imagine it, Rudy Marsh on the scrap heap."

I glared at him even harder and it took the last of my self control to not punch him in the face.

"You know," he continued, "when I first read these articles I actually had some sympathy for you. Yeah, despite all the stuff you've made me do I felt sorry for you. I thought maybe this would bring out some humanity in you, but maybe it's time for you to be put out to pasture. You're just a bitter guy and you're not going to get any better. Maybe it's for the best that you're letting yourself go. Be like a fat Elvis and become a joke."

I roared as I stood up and confronted him. I could feel anger pouring out of my eyes. My body was rigid with tension. My blood boiled. Hands were clenched either side of me, so tight I could feel my fingers digging into my palm.

"Better to be a has been than a never was. At least I amounted to something in my life, which is more than you'll ever do. I'm not going to let myself go. You think you know everything about me, but I know my body. I know what I can handle. You're not an expert in anything. You just think you know a lot because you've studied, but that's nothing compared to the real world. You're never going to be anything because you don't have a backbone. You don't have a spine. You're always going to be a coward, walking away whenever it gets rough."

"I'm not walking away now, am I? I'm right here, right in front of you, and you can get angry at me all you want but I don't care. When this is over you're going to go back to your team and ride out into the twilight, but I'll have what I needed. I'll forget you as quickly as that," he snapped his fingers. There was something about the gesture that triggered something inside me. I had already been rejected by Annette, and I was afraid that all my fans were going to forget me as well. Was it really going to be that easy for them? All this anger was festering inside me, spewing and simmering like an evil potion in a cauldron. But there was something about Josh in this moment that seemed different.

Showing me this rough and strong side impressed me. It was far better than anything he had shown me before.

The problem was that he didn't know when to stop.

"I know why you really came back here," he acted as though he had just come to some great realization. "I bet it's because you feel like you lost control. You know your career is coming to an end, don't you? You know that soon enough you're going to be just like the rest of us, trying to figure out our place in the world. I guess it must be hard to lose your grip on greatness, but that's just the way it has to go. Your time is almost up Rudy. The future is coming."

The future. The damned future. I didn't care about the future. Hell, I didn't care much for the present either, and I certainly didn't care about Josh. All I wanted to do in that moment was humiliate him. Tension burned inside me and I felt as though I was going to explode. Almost as soon as the words were out of his mouth everything flowed out of me and I hit him. My arm snapped back and then my fist cracked around his face. I felt the impact as I hit his jaw. He groaned and went flying backwards, for he hadn't been prepared for me to do this at all. He wasn't ready for the big bad world where anyone could hit you at any time. He was like a baby. I towered over him as he lay on the floor, looking shocked as he tended to his face. He touched his nose and his lip in case there was any blood, although I hadn't drawn any. Whatever bitter anger had been in his eyes had fled them. Now there was only fear. I liked it.

I strode towards him and grabbed him by the hair, making him wince as I pulled it. The power I had over this man almost made up for the fact that the rest of my life was in tatters. I hissed as I spoke, my breath like dragon's fire as I spoke. I wanted to do more to him. I wanted to show him that he couldn't dare speak to me like this. I wanted to make him regret ever deciding to work with me.

"Don't you dare speak to me like that again Josh. I wasn't lying when I said I can break you. I don't know why you've suddenly decided to come in here with all this confidence when you don't have the power to back it up. You're nothing compared to me. I have you in the palm of my hand and I can do whatever I like to you. I'll get you to do whatever the hell I want, and you're going to nod and do it like the obedient little puppy you are because that's what the world requires of you. You got that?"

He nodded, but I made the gesture more emphatic by forcing his head up and down. Tears were in his eyes. It was pathetic and pitiful, but there was something almost beautiful about it as well. With him I could take out all my frustrations about management, about Jesus Navarro, about Annette. Here was a man who had to do whatever I wanted, and it was such a liberating experience. I wanted to push him to his limits. I wanted to take him somewhere he had never been before. I wanted to... to... I wanted to show him I was serious.

I leaned down. Our faces were inches apart. I could smell his breath, and no doubt he could smell mine. His lips were full, his face clean shaven. His eyes were bright blue and his hair was the color of sand. He was younger than I, with the promise of the future still waiting to be fulfilled. This made me angry.

"Kiss me," I said. The words just slipped out of my mouth. I had no idea where they came from or why such a thought would form in my mind, but it was the only thing that seemed natural in the moment. Even Josh looked shocked.

"K-kiss you?" he stammered.

I tightened my grip on his head. "You heard me. I want you to understand that I can make you do anything Josh. And I want to know that you're going to obey me. So kiss me," I said.

I used my strength to pull his head closer towards me. He trembled as he nodded. He closed his eyes and I closed mine and then our lips met. It was the strangest sensation, and yet it was overwhelming as well. It felt as though, with this one gesture, I was taking control of my life back again. It felt as though I was giving the middle finger to all those people who were annoying me.

It felt good.

I hadn't expected him to taste so sweet, or for his lips to be so soft. I hadn't expected to actually enjoy it. The moment I felt a moan soar from my throat I pulled away and turned my back on him. I ordered him to leave, and moments later I heard the door slam behind me.

# Chapter Seven

Josh

I staggered out of the apartment, barely able to believe what had just happened. My head was still reeling from the strong blow Rudy had flung my way, but the pain had receded and been replaced by confusion. Even though it had just happened to me, I was still left with the question if it had really just happened. Had I just made out with Rudy Marsh? I walked a few paces away from the door and then I had to lean against the wall to steady myself. I hadn't intended to argue with him. All I wanted was to make peace with him, yet it seemed impossible. He always had a chip on his shoulder and just when I thought I had the upper hand, just when I thought I had some nugget of information that would turn the tides of power between us, he surprised me again. I guess I shouldn't have been surprised that he hit me considering his profession. He certainly knew how to throw a punch and I considered myself fortunate that nothing had been broken.

I would still have my looks, if nothing else.

But then the kiss happened. I had never been as terrified in all my life as I was in that moment when he had hold of my head and was shouting at me, his hot breath barraging me. I knew the balance of power wouldn't ever be equal between us, and I hated him for it. I hated him so much I could scream. Part of me was tempted to hammer on that door, to go back in there and ask him who the hell he thought he was to do something like that.

I know what answer I'd get though.

He's Rudy Marsh.

Some men can get away with doing the unthinkable. I pressed my fingers to my lips, feeling where he had kissed me. I thought it would have been like the rest of him, hard and bruising, and only designed to hurt. It had been tender. Warmth had slipped between my lips and a soft moan had emanated from the very depths of my soul. Up until this point I would never have thought that my best ever kiss would be with a guy, but I guess Rudy Marsh is no ordinary guy.

It left me confused though. What did it say about me that I enjoyed it this much?

I wasn't disgusted that I felt this way about kissing a guy. I felt disgusted because I had just kissed Rudy Marsh. The guy had treated me like crap and I shouldn't let him get away with this, but somehow it just seemed to happen. Somehow I had liked it and I even thought I might like to do it again.

God, what was wrong with me. I was like one of those naïve teenage girls who end up falling for the bad boy who cares nothing about them, just because they're cool and confident, and the girl thinks they can change them, or they have some self destructive behavior and don't believe they deserve anything more than to be mistreated. Is that what's going on here? Am I spiraling into a pit of self despair? Am I abusing myself by letting Rudy Marsh treat me this way?

I keep telling myself that I'm doing this for my career, that I'm paying my dues and once it's all over then it'll be worth it because I'll be able to go from strength to strength and use Rudy Marsh's recommendation as a spring board for my business. But is it really worth it to put up with all this? I'm sure that if anyone else came up to me and told me they were being treated this way I would tell them to get the hell out of dodge, but I guess maybe I don't care about myself as much as I care about other people. There's something dangerously magnetic about Rudy as well. He's like a tornado on the horizon. Even though you know he's destructive and dangerous there's a beauty about him as well. You find yourself transfixed, and you stand still, in awe of him until you realize that the storm is upon you and you're caught up in it completely.

*

Things weren't better the following day. I got up and showered, hoping that some sleep would have given me a better perspective on what had happened.

It hadn't.

I couldn't stop thinking about the kiss. I should have been thinking about the punch. I should have been on the phone to management about how Rudy was out of control, how he was drinking and hitting me and not acting like a good representative of the sport at all. I doubt they'd listen to me though. They did protect their athletes, as he said, and I would only be torpedoing my own chances of building my reputation. What I needed most of all, was to find some way to control Rudy, or at least show him I wouldn't always do what he wanted. He seemed to think he had this power over me that I couldn't resist. As much as I tried to prove to him that wasn't the case, the idea only became reinforced. I just couldn't break free and it annoyed me so much.

And then there was the kiss, the kiss that still played on my mind. The tender touch shouldn't have lingered in my thoughts so much, but it did. I hated myself for it. I hated myself for being so weak, and yet at the same time there was a flash of excitement when I thought about it. I couldn't deny that he was a handsome man, and I had never been shy of expressing my admiration for the human form. Was there something inside me that had just been awakened? None of my relationships had ever gone anywhere. Maybe it was because of this. But was Rudy gay as well?

I guess everyone has their secrets and it shouldn't surprise me if he was. After all, he's been living in a sports culture where he's drowning in machismo every minute of every day. He shares the locker room with warriors. It would almost be more surprising if he wasn't drawn to them. But as I thought about this it only brought about more questions, such as did he mean the kiss to be an affectionate one or was it just another way to display his power over me? Did he do it to torture me, to prove that he could get me to do anything? Did he enjoy it at all or did he just want to shock me?

There was only one man who would have these answers, and I knew they were not going to be forthcoming.

I went to the gym. This time I made sure that I was early. This time I told myself that I was going to have a say in how the session went. I breathed with relief when I realized I had arrived before Rudy. The last thing I needed was him holding my tardiness against me. While I waited, I browsed the latest sports news, thinking about Jesus Navarro. It must have been hard for Rudy to listen to news of his successor when for so long he had been top dog. It went some way to explaining his attitude, not that it excused his behavior. I had definitely touched a nerve the previous night when I mentioned that he was losing it. I had to make sure that if I decided to bring that up again I was standing farther away from him, to save my face from being clocked. I had a nasty bruise rising just underneath my left eye.

This time it was Rudy who was late.

"I thought you weren't going to show up," I said. He grunted at me and pushed past me, dumping his bag on the floor and heading straight to the treadmill. This isn't polite of me, but he looked like shit.

"Rudy, don't you have anything to say to me? If you can pull me up for being late when I was on time then what the hell do you call this?" I asked, trying to match his aggression in the hope that he would see me as something more than a wet blanket.

"I'm on time according to my schedule," he said, and started jogging at a good pace.

I had cowered before him when he punched me. I had no doubt that he saw the abject fear in my eyes because I had never been treated like this by anyone before. Every time I saw him I wanted to start anew. Every time I wanted to prove to him that I could stand toe to toe with him and endure the storm that whistled around me.

"That's not good enough. We need to stick to a routine. Do you think Jesus-"

I stepped back as I said this, which was a good idea as he turned around and glared at me.

"Don't you dare mention his fucking name again," Rudy said. His eyes were bloodshot. His stubble had grown, forming a dark shadow across his jaw. I noticed now that he was wearing the same shirt as he had been when I had been in the apartment. The scent of whiskey was unmistakable.

"Rudy. You've been drinking."

"So what?"

"So I don't think you're in a good state to exercise right now."

"That's what you think, but I know my body. I know what I'm capable of. I can prove you wrong. I can prove you all wrong."

I took a risk and stepped towards him. If he wasn't going to listen to reason then I had to try and think of something else that would get through that thick skull of his. "Rudy, if you're not worried about management hearing about you drinking then what are they going to think about you hitting me? What are they going to think about you kissing me? I'm betting that rumors of you being gay would make people at the gossip rags froth at the mouth."

"I'm not gay," he hissed in a low whisper, as though it was a sin.

"Then what happened last night? I think we should talk about it."

Rudy threw his head back and laughed. "Talk about it? You want to talk about it? That's all you want to do Josh, talk about things. Well some things you don't talk about. Some things you just get on with. I've had enough already. Today is not a day for exercise." He turned off the treadmill and hopped off, then returned to his bag. He rummaged around and ignored my pleas for him to stay and at least stick to some semblance of a routine, although he wasn't interested in any of that.

He rose and thrust a piece of paper in my hand.

"Here's a grocery list. Just drop it at the apartment and leave it outside the door. I don't particularly want to see your face for the rest of the day. I might turn up here tomorrow, or I might take a break for a few days. You're just going to have to wait and see."

"Rudy," I began, but he was already walking away. The man was impossible! I felt as though I was in some kind of strange world where the normal rules didn't apply. I couldn't imagine that anyone else in the entire world would act like Rudy was acting now, and I didn't know how to deal with him. Was I really supposed to just cope with all this until he left my life? Did I simply have to endure the storm until it disappeared across the opposite horizon?

*

My face was sullen as I went to the grocery store and pushed the cart around the aisles. I grabbed item after item off the shelf, annoyed that I was here doing menial tasks when I should have been helping Rudy to hone his body and become a fighting, fit machine. I didn't understand why he was being so lax with his fitness when he had the added threat of Jesus Navarro hovering over him. He said that he knew his body better than me, but there were still simple rules of nature that meant he would be suffering when the season began if he continued to neglect my advice.

I wondered if this was how doctors felt when they asked their patients to stop smoking or drinking and were met with empty promises. Empty promises were more than I was getting at the moment.

I walked around the store and ticked off everything on Rudy's list one by one. I stopped by the magazine rack when one of the magazine covers caught my eye. Rudy's image was on the front of it, in all his glory. His body was crouched low, his arms stretched back, his hands gripping the hockey stick, ready to shoot. His eyes were laser focused on the goal and there was nothing but determination etched upon his face. He might as well have been carved into a statue. The headline asked if this was going to be Rudy's best season ever, or if it was going to be the beginning of the end. I was flicking through the article when someone spoke to me.

"Excuse me, are you buying that? Do you mind if I have a quick look at it? I've just been searching and I think it's the last one they have," she said. She was a woman of medium height with long honey brown hair, and a kind face. I smiled.

"Sure thing," I said, and handed the magazine to her. She flipped it back over to the cover and chuckled to herself. I figured she was a fan. Most people in town were.

"I've seen his face on magazines over the years, and I never quite get used to it," she said.

"It feels like he's representing us in a way. Somehow seeing him on a magazine cover feels as though we're seeing ourselves." It was the way I had felt before I had actually met Rudy, but after the way he had treated me I didn't think I was going to worship him any longer. I wasn't going to let that stop me from being polite. Not saying anything nice about Rudy was going to be about as controversial as denying the existence of God in these parts.

"Yeah, that's a nice way of putting it. I knew him, back in the day. We used to see magazines like this and he would always joke that one day he would be on the cover. I never doubted him."

My ears pricked up at this. There were a lot of people who claimed they knew Rudy Marsh or had some personal connection with him. The amount of people who said he helped change their tires were countless, and made it sound as though Rudy was a full time mechanic. But there was something about this woman that had the ring of truth about it.

"I actually know him too. I'm his personal trainer. The name's Josh," I said, and held out my hand. She took it and replied that her name was

Annette. "You know, if you want a reunion I could probably organize one."

Annette smiled. "Actually we've already had one." The look in her eyes told me that it might not have gone to plan. "It's good to see him again after all these years. How is he in training? I hope you're pushing him hard."

"I'm trying to," I said. I hadn't been able to confide in anyone about the difficulties I'd been having, but with Annette I wondered if I had just found the perfect person to speak to. She knew Rudy. Surely she knew how obnoxious he could be? "Actually, to be honest with you I've been having a few problems with him. This might sound out of place, but could I buy you a cup of coffee? I'd like to pick your brain about him."

"Sure," Annette said.

We paid for our groceries and then went into the adjoining café. It smelled of freshly baked goods, and the pungent aroma of coffee hung in the air. I grabbed a smoothie, while Annette had a hot chocolate.

"So what did you want to ask me about? I'm not sure I can be of much use. I haven't heard from Rudy for years before he returned here."

"To be honest it's just good to talk to someone who knows him. I haven't dared speak about this with anyone else because I know what it's like when you say something bad about him," I lowered my voice to a conspiratorial whisper as I knew that ears were always listening out for any controversial statements.

Annette leaned back and laughed. "Oh yes, I know that all too well. I guess a lot of people forget that he's a real person. They just see the star, and it blinds them to the reality of the situation. I've had to struggle with that myself. We meant a lot to each other in high school and then he went off to pursue his hockey career. It hurt me, but over the years people have always been curious about the girl he left behind. I've had to put on a brave face and tell them that I have no regrets and that I'm proud of all he's accomplished in his career. I can't tell them how much he hurt me or how much I cried, because that's not the story they want to hear. It's not about me, it's all about him. I'm just a supporting character," as she said this her gaze darted away and I got a real sense of melancholy from her. I understood the feeling though. I felt the same way. In Rudy Marsh's world the only thing that truly mattered was Rudy Marsh himself. Other people's feelings barely registered on his radar.

"But that's all in the past now," she said with a forced smile. "And I'm sure you didn't come here to talk about this. What can I do for you?"

"Well, it is to do with that really. It's Rudy he's... he's being incredibly difficult. When I got the job to work with him I was over the moon. But it's like he doesn't want to listen to me. He never takes my advice and he's been threatening to blackball me if I tell anyone what he's like. He just expects me to sit back and let him do what he wants rather than doing my job. I'm only starting out with this, but I'm trying to have pride in my profession and I don't want my first client to return to his team being so unfit and out of shape. Rudy might give me a good recommendation, but everyone is going to see the state of him and they're going to ask what happened, and it's all going to come back to me. I need him to take this seriously."

"That's the problem with Rudy. He only ever does what he wants to do, and everything else can go to hell," Annette said with more than a hint of bitterness in her voice. I shouldn't have been surprised. She hadn't told me explicitly that she and Rudy had dated in high school, but it wasn't hard to put two and two together. Love at that age was usually intense and it was clear that it still meant a lot to her now. I could imagine her collapsing into tears after Rudy left because Rudy was the kind of man who left a trail of destruction in his wake.

"But why? What made him like this?" I asked.

Annette took a sip of her drink before she answered. "I don't think it's any one thing. From a young age he was great at hockey. He used to play against guys who were two age brackets up from him and he used to destroy them. There was always a hardness to Rudy, like nothing was going to get in his way. I think a long time ago someone told him that if he was going to be a great hockey player then he had to sacrifice everything else along the way, and that's just what he's done. I don't think he's incapable of love or caring about other people, he's just never trained that side of himself. Maybe there's someone out there who can bring out that side of him. There was a time when I thought it was me."

I pitied her for loving a man who could never have loved her back the way she wanted, or the way she deserved. I suppose I couldn't blame her for feeling that way either. Rudy was the kind of guy anyone could fall in love with. He was strong, handsome, and he had that kind of animal magnetism that was all too rare. I caught myself before I lost myself in my own thoughts. Images flashed in my mind, of the two of us face to face with barely an inch between us, of my hands on his flesh as I gave him a massage, and I had to stop myself from thinking about these things. He was in my head and it confused me.

"So how am I supposed to make him do what's best for him? How am I supposed to train him if he's adamant that he knows best?"

Annette sighed. "I don't know. I'm sorry I can't be more help. The only thing I can say is that Rudy must be scared right now. He's spent his life in hockey and now he's starting to realize that it's not going to be there all the time. He's going to have to change, and it's going to take a strong person to make him see that. I wasn't strong enough to be that person. Maybe if you train him you can get through to him. You might even need to go to the team and tell them what's been going on."

"If I do that then Rudy will just tell them that I've failed him," I said.

Annette shrugged. "At the end of the day Rudy knows what's best for him. He's not going to jeopardize his career for the sake of his stubbornness. Just keep on at him. Eventually he'll come around."

I wasn't sure how true her words were. From what I'd seen of Rudy up until now he didn't seem like he was going to come around at all, but at least it was good to know his attitude to me wasn't entirely personal. A large part of it was due to his personality, and there wasn't anything I could do to change that.

# Chapter Eight

Rudy

I know it wasn't the best thing to do, but I couldn't help myself. I sat there and watched all the news stories about Jesus Navarro. They were packed with highlights of his exploits and his talent, and I hated how easy he made the game look. He slalomed through players as though they weren't there and it wasn't difficult to see why management wanted someone like him. I knew it was just business, but this business was more than that to me. It was my life, and I wasn't about to let it end with a whimper. I stretched out my muscles and felt a slight twinge. Maybe Josh was right and I had been overdoing it on the weights. It was hard to admit that he was good at his job, not that I would ever tell him that to his face.

God, I had so much anger inside me and I don't know where it's all going to go. I wish I could just go back in time without all this glitz and glamor where the only thing that mattered was the game. It seemed so much easier back then when things were simpler, or maybe I'm just getting jaded.

It still hurt that Annette didn't think we could be something together. I always figured I could come back here and pick up where I left off, but I guess it's never that easy.

I was sitting there in the dark, wondering how I was going to handle things. I felt the light dwindling. Whether I had two seasons left or five, or however many, I knew they weren't going to be endless. Eventually I was going to have to hang up my boots and if there was one thing I knew more than anything else, it was that I wanted to go out on my own terms.

But how was that?

I'd known other players that had outstayed their welcome. They had all been unwilling to listen to their bodies and they had been shamed by younger, quicker players. They had all tarnished their legacies by hanging around and being humiliated, shells of their former selves. I wanted to go out on top, when I was still a champion. If Jesus Navarro was going to take my place then it was only because I had left it empty, not because he had wrested it from me. But to do that I needed to be in better shape than I had ever been in before, and for that I needed Josh's help.

It was with reluctance that I picked up the phone and called him.

"Josh," I barked, not wanting to let him relax.

"What is it Rudy?" he asked. The tension in his voice didn't escape my notice. It was clear that he had enmity towards me and I didn't blame him after the way I had treated him, but a little bit of tension was good for the soul. I remember a guy I had a great partnership with on the ice, Darren Huckerby, now that was a bastard of a guy that I hated with every fiber of my being, but damn if we didn't have a great time out on the ice. Nobody could stand in our way. Maybe the same could be true for Josh and I.

"I want you to come over here. I have a bit of a niggle."

"Can't we deal with it at our next session? It's getting kind of late," Josh said.

"Oh, I see how it is. The moment I actually want to do some training is the moment you're going to quit on me? Is that really how you want to play this Josh?"

Josh sighed. I could almost imagine him weighing up the possibilities in his mind. Should he give in to my whims again or should he try and show me that he wasn't going to be pushed around?

"Fine. I'll be there soon," he said.

A smile twitched on my face. I still had power over him, and he was foolish if he thought that he could ever hit back against me.

It didn't take him long to arrive. I was just wearing pajama slacks and a vest. I had a lamp on, which illuminated the room in a soft amber glow. Josh walked up, huffing and puffing, with his massage table. I watched him set it up in the middle of the room.

"So are you actually saying that I was right to advise you to not go so heavy on the weights?" he asked.

I wasn't about to give him that much credit. "Actually I think I strained something while I was showering," I said.

Josh just laughed. I guess he didn't believe me, but I didn't particularly care. He was just another guy that I was going to put up walls with. It's what I did. Annette was proof of that. If I had been more open with her over the years then maybe things would be different. Maybe she would take me back. There's something about Josh that just gets under my skin. I'm not sure what it is, but he drives me crazy.

"Alright then, where does it hurt the most?" he asked.

"Right in the middle of my back, but while you're here you might as well do everywhere. It's been a while since I've had a proper massage. I don't want my muscles to get too tight."

"Sure thing," Josh said grudgingly. I pulled off my vest and lay down on the massage table, resting my head in the open hole. I let my arms hang down. Josh squirted some lotion on his hands and began to rub along my shoulder blades and down my spine, gradually reaching everywhere along my back. His fingers were magic and I had to give him credit where it was due; he's a damn good masseuse and I could feel the tension oozing off of me. He rubbed the back of my neck and pinched my skin in certain places where it felt as though it was going to hurt, but the pain was just on the right side of pleasure.

Soft moans burst out of my mouth as he worked on my body, easing the tension out of my muscles. He was stronger than he looked. I could feel all the strength in his hands, gripping me and kneading me, driving out all the aches and pains that had gathered within.

"You're really carrying a lot of tension around. Are you sure you aren't more upset about all this stuff with Jesus Navarro?" Josh asked.

I rolled my eyes. "I told you that I don't want to talk about it. This Navarro guy is just the latest in a long line of people who are coming, trying to take my crown, and they're not going to succeed. I know what

I'm doing and I'm still at the top of my game. He can come and try to succeed where others have failed, but I'll see off his challenge and he can go crying back to where he belongs because he doesn't have what it takes to take me out."

"If you say so," Josh said.

I grimaced and was glad that he couldn't see the expression on my face. I sighed before I started speaking. "But I have to admit that I've been thinking about what we're doing together. I think I'm ready to step it up."

"I see," Josh said. Although I couldn't see his face I could hear the smugness in his voice. It didn't really matter what he thought. As long as he did his job and got me fit then he could think what he liked. He might well believe that I was scared of Jesus Navarro's challenge, but that didn't mean he was right.

Even though he was.

Slightly.

But I wasn't going to admit that to him.

"I'm glad you've seen the light. Thankfully I've got a few good exercise regimes ready to go. I'm sure you'll find them challenging and rewarding, although you're going to have to go harder than you might want to at first to make sure you make up for all the time we've lost."

"Sure, whatever. I'm getting bored of sitting around in the apartment anyway. It'll do me good to get out of here for a while."

"Being at home hasn't been as good as you thought it would be?" Josh asked. Something about the way he asked the question made my ears prick up, but I wasn't sure what he was getting at.

"Not exactly. To be honest I'm a little unsure about why I came back here in the first place. I guess I thought maybe I'd find a piece of myself that I left behind, but it's not always that simple. Coming back here... I don't know. People change, things change. You start to wonder how much you've changed as well. Sometimes you can spend so much time away from a place that you lose your connection to it."

"I wouldn't have assumed that was the case after what happened at the bar. People there worshiped you, and you looked like you loved it."

"Don't get me wrong I'm grateful for the fans here. I know I mean a lot to them and when they look at me they see someone who managed to break free of this place and make something of themselves, but I'm always going to be a little like a stranger to them. I had a life here and I thought I might be able to come back to that life from where I left off, but I can't. I'm starting to see that I have to make a big effort to make my last years in the game good ones, and then when I can retire maybe I can settle back here. Maybe I'm still caught in between two lives."

"Well I'm glad you're starting to think about things like this. I guess maybe Annette was right, you are going to do what's best for you," Josh said.

At first what he said barely registered, but then I realized he'd mentioned Annette's name. I propped myself up on my elbows and lifted my head from its crevice.

"What are you talking about? How do you know Annette?"

"Oh, uh, well, I just happened to run into her at the store. It was funny really, we were both looking at the same magazine with an article about you and we got to talking. She's a nice woman, very friendly, she helped to give me some insight about you."

"Insight? You went to her and got some fucking insight? What the hell are you thinking? This is some creepy behavior," I glared at Josh and he immediately looked on edge.

"It wasn't anything like that, honest. We just ran into each other and she seemed like she could use someone to talk to. We didn't spend that much time with each other. It was just a funny coincidence, I promise."

He cowered before me, as if I was going to throttle him. To be honest the thought crossed my mind. I wasn't proud of it, but this was hitting too close to the mark. I liked to keep my worlds separate. I had succeeded for many years in maintaining two different lives, but now that I had returned here the lines between them were blurring and now there was a distinct crossover. The last thing I wanted was for Josh to be gossip buddies with Annette. She knew me better than anyone else and the things she might tell him... the thought was enough to make me shudder.

I curled my lip and snarled at him. "What you did was unprofessional. I don't want you speaking to her again. You're my personal trainer. That's all. That doesn't give you an excuse to rummage around my personal life, you got that?"

"I didn't mean anything by it Rudy, I promise. It was honestly just a funny thing that happened. I didn't plan to see her again, but the truth is I feel like I needed some insight because of the way you've been acting. All I've been trying to do is help you and you keep treating me like shit. I want to help you be the best athlete you can be, but you chew me out at every opportunity. It's not fair."

"Yeah, well, life isn't fair so you'd better get used to it. If I'm the worst client you ever have then you should consider yourself lucky. I've already told you that I'll do your stupid regimes so just take comfort in that fact and carry on with your massage. I'm tired of talking to you. You're not my friend. Just see to my body, that's all."

Josh muttered something under his breath as I turned back to the table and placed my head back where it belonged. I didn't catch what he said, though I assumed it wasn't complimentary. The fact that he had seen Annette really got to me. I'm not sure why it affected me this much. Maybe it was because I wasn't ready for my worlds to collide. Maybe it was because I didn't want Josh knowing the real me. But why should that frighten me? It wasn't as though he meant anything to me. He was just some trainer that I would chew up and spit out before too much time had passed.

My entire body was tense as he kept massaging me. I was thinking about the future and what would happen after hockey, how I would have to spend my life like this if Annette wasn't going to let me back into her heart. Was I going to be so sad as to live in some apartment with the TV blaring out just so that I could pretend I had some company? God, the way his hands worked my muscles felt so good. I moaned softly as his fingers worked their way down my spine, all the way to the base of my back. He found a particularly sore spot that just ached so much and when he touched me it felt as though all the pain was flooding out of my body. I nodded and begged him to keep touching there, which I hated because I didn't want to seem desperate, but he was damn good at his job.

He pressed the sore spot and I felt the tension unwinding throughout my body, as though he had thrown some switch and everything was unspooling. My limbs went limp and I felt as though I was melting. I hadn't felt this good or this relaxed in forever. Tingles spread through me, and that was when I realized I was enjoying the massage far too much. I tried to fight it at first, but there was no fighting something like this. It was stupid to think about because this was Josh and he wasn't a remarkable guy, but there was something about the way he touched me that awakened my desire. I could feel the throbbing arousal stretching through my body, expanding, making me bigger and harder and everything that a man should be.

"Do my legs," I ordered. I guess part of it was the fact that I had so much power over him. There wasn't anything that he could do to resist me. I'd proven time and time again that he was willing to do whatever I said, and I was really eager to find out just how far I could push him. My throat ran dry and my heart started hammering inside as his hands ran down my legs, pushing my slack pants up. His hands ran up my muscles and squeezed tightly. I felt them run up my thigh, his fingers curling around the huge toned muscles, getting closer and closer to the part of me where all the energy was focused, where all the strength and all the vigor was held. It felt so hot I wouldn't have been surprised if it was glowing.

Murmuring breath slipped through my lips as I felt myself twitching. I wasn't sure if he was aware how the blood was flowing through my body or how I was feeling, but he soon would be.

I rolled my hips around and there was no doubt he saw the huge bulge stretching my pants. I looked up at him, meeting his gaze. The color drained from his face and his gaze darted between my eyes and my cock. He stared at the bulge. I arched my eyebrows, feeling cocky and confident.

"Suck me off," I said.

He stared at me open mouthed. "I... I'm not gay," he protested. I didn't give a fuck whether he was gay or not.

"I'm hard. I need to release this tension and you're the one that's going to help me. You're the one massaging me. Take care of it," I said, enunciating those last few words to make him understand that there was no choice in the matter. He was doing this whether he liked it or not. This was the final way in which I was truly going to show him who was in control here. I was going to make him my little slut and he was going to love every minute of it.

Yeah.

I bet Jesus fucking Navarro couldn't do this.

Josh stared at it for what seemed like an eternity. The frustration and the tension were still keeping me aroused, but if he didn't do something about it then I was going to lose it and that was not going to happen. After all the crap I'd had to put up with I needed to get my kicks from somewhere and Josh was the man to help me. With one hand I slipped the pants away, pulling them down to expose myself, and with the other I grabbed Josh's wrist and shoved his hand down towards my cock, moaning softly as his flesh met mine.

# Chapter Nine

Josh

I gaped open mouth when I saw it, when I saw him. The conversation had taken an unusual turn. When I had mentioned Annette I thought he was going to kick my ass. I couldn't say for sure whether I would have preferred that to what else he had in mind. I kept telling myself that I wasn't gay. I already told Rudy, not that he seemed to care. I didn't think he was gay either, he just had something that he needed to take care of and I was the only one in the immediate vicinity. It was fucking humiliating though, to know that he could order me to do anything and I would do it. In the back of my mind I was saying that I needed to tell him no, that I could just walk away.

Before the threat of him giving me a bad recommendation was enough to keep me hanging on. I wish I could say that this was the case on this occasion, but it wasn't.

The truth was that I wanted him.

I don't know what it was that switched within me. I don't know if I had these latent feelings all my life and Rudy was only bringing them out now, or if it was purely because it was Rudy Marsh himself that I was attracted to rather than men in general, but I fucking wanted him. Everything went tight in my body and I could feel the breath dripping from my mouth. When he grabbed my wrist my heart skipped a beat and when I felt him I wasn't filled with revulsion or a sense that I needed to get as far away from him as possible. My hands curled around him and I loved the feeling of his taut, warm skin in the palm of my hand. I knew it was wrong. Everything inside my head was telling me that this wasn't me, that I wasn't supposed to be here doing this, but there was something else stirring inside my heart and I just knew that I wanted to be close to him.

Looking at him was to see the ideal form of a man. He was oiled from where I had been massaging him, and if I'm honest with myself then I have to say that I felt these stirrings while I had been rubbing him up and down. To feel the contours of his muscles and really dig into his skin was to drown in an expanse of warm and exciting flesh, to feel the yearning touch of another man. I could have easily fallen into him and swam in the sea of his masculinity because it was so inviting, so magnetic. I honestly felt like my life wouldn't be the same if I didn't take this opportunity. My hands felt blessed for being able to touch him, as though I was one of god's chosen flock. I'll never forget the feeling of his tight muscles under my fingers, or the way his body seemed formed to be absolutely perfect. I was in good shape myself, but Rudy was on another level.

And then there was his cock.

When I saw his bulge I was impressed by his size. I guess I shouldn't have been. To have the cocky confidence of Rudy it was natural that he should have been hung like a fucking horse. I gulped in a mixture of fear and anticipation as he exposed himself, his cock throbbing with all its power. I ran my hand up and down the long shaft, feeling my fingers curl around the rippling veins that gave it its strength. The tip was smooth and round, and it was as though it winked at me. I was overwhelmed inside by the sheer force of it all. It felt as though I had been hit with thunder and lightning and I was still caught in the eye of the storm. My mouth was hanging open, but I couldn't say anything. I just kept staring at him, wondering if this was really happening or if this was some intense dream that I would wake up from soon.

But there was no mistaking this for a dream. I knew that he wouldn't feel this real in anything other than reality. He was hot, scorching hot, and sweat began to pepper my brow and flow underneath my clothes. His grip was firm on my wrist and he held me there, making it clear that I wasn't free to go until I'd done what he wanted.

"I told you to suck me off," he said in that grizzled, demanding tone of his. It was a tone that I had hated so much ever since I had met him. I didn't know what he had done to me, but now it was beginning to turn me on. I kind of liked the idea of being anything he wanted, even though he had been my enemy. I felt myself bending down, being pulled by his sheer force of will, and I ended up breathing in the manly musk that sizzled around his cock. I opened my mouth. My lips were trembling. It got bigger and bigger as I got closer and closer. I could feel Rudy laughing.

This was all a big joke to him. A way to humiliate me. Well, I was going to show him that this wasn't a joke. I was going to show him that I could meet whatever challenge he was going to throw my way. If he was going to try and degrade me then I was going to show him what I was made of.

I was going to prove to him that I could give the best damn blow job.

I summoned all the courage I had and let my hand drop down to the thicket of dark hair at the base of his cock. I rubbed it up and down. There was still some lotion on my hands so it made his cock nice and wet. The rest of his body was oiled as well, like some Greek Adonis. Then my lips met him. It was my first time ever tasting a cock. It was hot and heavy and the taste filled my mouth. I slowly let myself fall over him, taking him deeper and deeper into my mouth. I stretched my jaws to take all of him and let my tongue slide around. The sweet taste of the oil contrasted with the burning, heavy taste of his flesh, but it was all delicious and I found that I couldn't get enough.

His hand left my wrist and rested against the back of my head. He clutched a fistful of my hair and held me tightly. Pain and pleasure burned through me, blurring together in a haze. I started to suck on his tip and when I heard him moan it was music to my ears. I brought my head back and forth, and when I came down he used his strength to hold me there, making me choke on every inch of his cock. I felt him pressing against the back of my throat and my mouth was full of him. When he allowed me to pull away I gasped in air, and as my mouth opened, a waterfall of saliva drizzled out, gushing over him. It dripped down the long towering shaft and I was barely able to catch my breath before I was on him again, this time by choice.

I gorged myself on him, licking him up and down, leaving trailing kisses all over his shaft before I took him into my mouth again and sucked hard, so hard the world was a blur of movement. I twisted my head to the side and let it loll in his lap, pressing his cock against the wall of my cheek, stretching it so hard I thought it was going to rip my face apart. I looked up at him and saw the tension on his face. I listened to his moans and I knew that he was enjoying it.

Yes.

I could bring Rudy Marsh to his knees. I could prove to him that I was more than what he thought.

I could make him come.

I flicked the tip with my tongue and brought my hands up and down at the same time. Rudy pushed me off and swung his body around so that he was sitting on the table, with his legs hanging down. I moved so that I was on my knees. God he towered above me, so tall, every muscle on display and I couldn't get enough. I had never felt anything this exhilarating before. Bells were ringing in my mind and my body was ablaze. Sweat dripped down from every pore and I didn't care that I was humiliating myself. I didn't care that he was treating me like some dirty whore. All I cared about was the hard cock that was in my mouth and being smeared over my face.

I was locked in the heat between his thighs as he kept his hands pressed against my head, holding me tightly against him so I barely had room to breathe. My tongue lolled out of my mouth like a panting dog and I felt proud that he was this hard because of me.

"I guess you're not completely useless after all," he said. He grabbed my head and pulled me up again, commanding me to my feet. My knees were weak and I felt unsteady, but I was able to remain upright.

"Let's see how you're feeling," Rudy added, reaching out to grab my crotch. I groaned as he fondled my cock, feeling how hard it was. I never thought that sucking Rudy Marsh off would turn me on this much but it had, and now he was touching me. I was either in heaven or hell, and I didn't care which.

He pulled my clothes away and spat on his hand, then jerked me off a little. Then he took his hand away.

"Play with yourself," he said.

I stood there in the middle of his apartment and did what he asked without questioning him. I jerked off, my hand moving quickly, staring at his naked body. His cock still dripped wet from when I had sucked him and I longed to taste him again. The heat lingered against my lips and sizzled on my tongue. I wanted him badly. I wanted him more than I had wanted anything else in my entire life and I hated myself for it. I was ashamed, degraded, utterly humiliated that I could be turned on like this for someone who was supposed to be my enemy, but now I realized I wanted him as my lover.

I reached out for him with my free hand, only for it to be slapped away.

Oh Rudy, you are a cruel master.

I moaned and whimpered as I could feel the heat running through me and all the pent up pleasure threatening to burst out. Rudy could see this etched all over my face. He laughed, a taunting, mocking laugh, but I knew he couldn't make fun of me any longer. I was doing exactly what he wanted. I was making him hard, and I was succeeding.

"You're going to come aren't you? You're going to come like a little bitch," he said.

I stammered out something. I could barely form a coherent thought because I had so many other things rampaging through my mind and my body. Something dormant had been awakened, something dark and delicious that left me delirious and dazed. I could feel it roiling within me, as though it was going to break free and tear my body asunder. I should have been scared, but all I wanted was to feel it. All I wanted was to feel what was bristling and bursting and he was right. It was coming. It was coming so hard and I wasn't sure I could stop it.

"Come for me Josh," he said. "Get down on the floor and come."

I fell to the floor, sinking down where I lay and played with myself, looking up at him as though he was on Olympus. I never took my eyes off him as I brought myself to climax. My face twisted and the maelstrom within my heart raged as he commanded me, and I followed his order. It came exploding out in a hot jet and it splattered all over my hand and stomach, the hot drops thick and viscous and creamy. I felt empty, drained. My chest heaved and my heart hammered.

And Rudy wasn't done with me yet.

He had that smug smirk on his face as he dropped to the floor and grabbed my head. I was limp and aching and the last drops were being squeezed out of my dick.

"I told you I wanted something and now I'm going to get it," he said as he thrust me in between his thighs. I was hanging off his hard cock again. I was so weak I could do nothing as he fucked my face and I took it. He hammered the back of my mouth and I felt all the heat dripping over my tongue. I looked up and watched his face twist in fury, knowing that I was the one who made him feel like this, that I was the one who brought Rudy Marsh to the cusp of an orgasmic climax, and then he threw his head back and roared. The moment he did so I felt the hot stream of cum in my mouth, flowing over my tongue and into the back of my throat. I choked on him and took everything he had to give me, guzzling down the last drops of his pleasure because it was mine, all mine.

He took his cock away and turned to lean on the massage table. I gasped to catch my breath, still reeling from everything that had just happened. My body trembled and tingled and I felt as though I was going to faint. My vision was blurred. The only thing that was clear was Rudy.

I staggered up, slowly and gradually regaining my strength. My breaths were deep. His taste lingered in my mouth. I groaned and wiped sweat from my brow. I reached out to him. My hand was barely inches away from his skin when he suddenly spoke without turning.

"Get out," he said in a dry drawl.

I couldn't believe my ears. I was stunned, paralyzed. I couldn't believe what I was hearing.

"Get out!" he repeated, this time almost yelling. My mind was a whirl and I had no idea what to do, but given how he had always treated me before, I understood that he could be angry, so all I wanted was to get out of there. I raced out of his apartment and slammed the door behind me. As I dragged my feet underneath me I started to sob and cry and I choked on my tears. I thought I was so pathetic. I hated myself because I realized something. As much as I hated what he did to me, I didn't hate Rudy Marsh. I fucking loved him and I had no idea how to handle my feelings.

# Chapter Ten

Rudy

I stood there against the massage table, naked, sweat dripping from every pore. The moment had been intense and everything had just happened without me realizing it. Instead of torturing Josh I had done something else, something that affected me deeply. My chest heaved and my mind was still reeling from everything that happened. I was filled with frustration and anger and I had no idea what was going to happen next between us, if anything was going to happen. I stormed to the bathroom and turned the faucet on the shower, hoping that the warm water would cleanse the ache in my soul. It didn't take long for steam to rise and the entire room was filled in a mist. I stepped into the shower and closed my eyes, feeling the hot drops pepper my flesh. I turned around, allowing the water to reach every part of me, and then I slammed my fists against the wall.

I had never considered myself to be gay. I didn't think I should be feeling this way about someone like Josh either. He was a nobody, and yet the way he had made me feel... fuck! It had been just about the best damned orgasm in my entire life. The way he sucked and touched me... it was as though his hands and his mouth were magic. The power I had over him drove me crazy and I couldn't stop thinking about it. He looked so good hanging off the end of my cock, and the way he let me do so many things to him... fuck I loved it and now I wasn't sure what to do.

This was supposed to be a way to punish and torture him, but in the end I was the one who was tortured. It made me think of things that I would rather forget as well. There was a tight ball in the pit of my stomach and I couldn't seem to get the knot undone. Part of me hated myself for the way I had told him to leave as well. I knew that I was immature and I couldn't handle my emotions, but I didn't care. Or maybe I did. God why is everything so damned complicated? All I want is to play hockey. Out there on the ice everything is so simple. I just skate and shoot and I win. It makes sense. The real world, the outside world, that has never been easy for me. All these feelings and emotions and desires aren't something that I've been used to and I wish I could make them make sense, but somehow there's always something that's getting in the way.

The water dripped down my body in thick rivulets. I squeezed some liquid soap into my hands and rubbed it all over my body, watching the foam rise and froth and slide down. It couldn't cleanse the ache in my heart though. I closed my eyes and tried to lose myself to the rhythm of the water. There were shadows in my mind and I started to peer into them. I tried to look away, I tried to forget these dark things, but somehow they were always there, torturing me, haunting me. I slipped down to my knees as the water poured all around me and I began to weep. The tears were lost in the pouring water and I hid from the world. I hid because I was a damned coward and I didn't know how to handle these feelings that were so intense.

*

I cleaned myself up and got myself composed. I dressed, but when I returned to the lounge I was faced with the area where Josh had sucked me off. I let myself be weak. I had given into my wild desires and I knew I should have been stronger. I breathed deeply and closed my eyes. There was only one person who could help me now, although she might not want to see me.

It was late at night. The moon was high in the sky, hanging like a flat puck. I used to stare up at it and wonder how far I could hit it. I walked up to Annette's door and hammered my fist against it. A light was on in the bedroom. She always had a tendency to stay up late. She said she liked the way the night felt. It was calm and quiet, and somehow everything seemed to make more sense than it did in the light.

When she opened the door and saw me she didn't seem surprised. "What do you want Rudy?" she asked with a sigh.

"I need to talk to you," I said.

"Look, I know that being back here probably brings up a lot of memories, but that doesn't mean you can just come around whenever you please. It's late. You should be at home."

"There are plenty of places I should be, but I'm not. I'm here. Are you going to let me in or not?" I asked.

Annette sighed and then stepped back, allowing me to enter.

"You know you can't always do this. I'm only letting you in because we have a history, and because I know you're not going to be around here forever."

"I think you should be a little nicer to me. After all, I found out today that you've been gossiping about me behind my back."

"What are you talking about?" she asked.

"Josh," I said, glaring at her before I went to sit down on her couch. "I heard about the little conversation you had in the store."

"I never said anything bad about you."

"It's not the fact that you said anything bad, it's the fact that you thought it was a good idea to say anything at all."

"Josh seemed nice, and he was struggling. I don't know why you're so hard on him. He only wants the best for you. He seems like he knows what he's talking about. Maybe you should give him a chance and listen to him. It might do you some good if you're so worried about your future."

I snorted and shook my head, huffing loudly and exhaling deeply. Annette was one of the few people who could actually endure my temper tantrums. I had to admire her patience, although when I was lost in the moment I wasn't giving much thought to praising anyone.

"If you're here to talk about what you wanted to talk about before I should let you know that my feelings haven't changed. You know we can't go back in time," she said.

"I'm not here to talk about that," I said. My tone softened as I leaned forward and clasped my hands in between my legs. "I know that I'm difficult sometimes. It can't be easy. I appreciate you letting me in."

Annette smiled. "I appreciate that. After all we've been through there's not much else I can do really. What's on your mind Rudy? I know that something is troubling you. Is it all this business with the player your team is trying to sign?"

I shook my head. "Something happened between Josh and me."

Annette looked shocked. "What do you mean something happened? Did you have a fight? Oh Rudy, you didn't get angry at him because he spoke to me, did you? It's not his fault. You really have to watch what you're doing with him. He doesn't deserve that. He's just trying to do his job."

"We didn't fight," I said. "It was something else. The same thing that happened with Cody." The moment I mentioned Cody's name she stiffened. It was a name that was rarely mentioned between us, and I never liked to think of him too much because it was too painful. I hated bringing him up because I could see the sorrow swimming in her eyes.

"Oh. I see." She said, taking a moment to compose herself. "I didn't think that was something you were still interested in."

"I didn't either. And now I'm confused."

"You know this isn't easy for me to talk about," Annette said.

"I know, and I'm sorry, but there's nobody else I can talk about this with."

"Haven't you ever told anyone else?"

I shook my head. "I thought that I could run from it or that it would sort itself out."

Annette looked shocked, although she kept her tone gentle. It's part of the reason why I loved her. She never made me feel as though I was strange for feeling the way I felt. She was the one person in all the world who could understand me, and I knew my life would have been a hell of a lot easier had I just been able to love her in the way she wanted, in the way she needed.

"You never... got close with anyone? Not even people who were on the same team as you?"

"I couldn't allow myself to do that. I know what people would think, how they would gossip. I didn't want it to affect my career. The only thing I wanted was for people to know that I was a great hockey player. Anything else was just unnecessary. But I couldn't allow myself to get close to people. The locker room it's... I mean, we've all got each other's back to a certain extent, but there are some people who are only out for themselves. I couldn't allow myself to be so weak. I needed to try and keep this part of my life private. I thought I had it under wraps and under control. All I wanted was to play hockey."

"Have you ever thought that this is why you get so temperamental? Bottling all this stuff up inside can't be good for you Rudy. Maybe you should think about seeing a therapist."

"I'm not seeing a shrink," I dismissed with a glare.

Annette sighed. "Well you need to do something because you clearly can't carry on like this. And the thing is, Rudy, as much as you mean to me, I can't always be the one you run to when you need to talk about this stuff. I'm not sure it's possible to leave the past behind like you want to. It might be time to start talking about it with someone else."

"Like Josh?" I said.

Annette smiled. "He does seem like he's made an impression on you, and he's stuck around longer than most people would have. If you've had this experience with him then maybe you owe it to him to tell him the truth. He must be so confused right now. What did you do after it happened?"

I squirmed with shame. "I told him to get out."

"Oh, Rudy," Annette said, and I felt guilt swim through my heart. "You need to go and talk to him. He needs to know that he's not at fault here. Think of what he's going through right now. The only problem with cutting yourself off from the rest of the world and focusing on hockey, is that you forget the rest of us have emotions too. Rudy, as much as you would like it to be otherwise you're not living in this world alone. Nobody is. You have to figure out what makes you happy otherwise you're always going to be this volatile, and you're not going to have the outlet of hockey to help you."

"I know. I know," I said. In some ways I had known that I was going to have to talk with Josh about what happened, but I guess I needed Annette to confirm it. "I've spent so long running from what happened, it's hard to face it again."

"Is that why you stayed away for so long?" Annette asked.

I nodded. "One of the reasons, anyway. When I was out there playing hockey I could pretend that this was another life. I didn't have to worry about ever coming back here, but recently I've been thinking about the future and I guess it's just been on my mind. You know that I'm... I'm sorry for what happened before."

"Rudy, we've been over this again and again. You don't have to apologize. It's water under the bridge. But look, I hope that one day you can come back here and you can be happy here because I'd love to have you around more. I've missed having you in my life. You're a good friend and I want you to be happy. Go and talk to Josh. I think it will do you some good to open up to him. I've got a feeling you can trust him."

She rose from her seat and came over to me. She leaned down and hugged me. Her hair flowed across my face like a veil and I allowed myself to sink into her embrace.

"I don't deserve you," I said.

"I know," Annette replied. I nodded and rose from her couch, knowing that I needed to do as she said if I was ever going to wrench these feelings out of my heart. But talking to Josh was going to be about the hardest thing I had ever done. I left Annette's company and sat in my car for a while before I headed out to Josh's place. When I arrived I sat in my car for a little while longer, delaying the inevitable. I leaned against the head rest and closed my eyes, trying to figure out how some parts of my life could be such a mess. On the ice I was a god, but every other aspect of my life was a mess and it was all because of what happened with Cody. I let out a dry laugh, hating myself for being so weak that something that happened a lifetime ago could still affect me so much.

I turned off the engine and stepped out of the car, forcing myself to walk to Josh's door. It would have been easy to walk away and leave this all behind, but I was done being a coward. I had run away once before and it hadn't done me any good. Things needed to change.

I knocked on the door. Josh answered and he looked like hell. There were dark shadows under his eyes and they were bleary. Clearly he had been crying. I felt ashamed for the pain I had caused him, especially when he hadn't done anything to deserve it. Perhaps things would have been different if he had stood up for himself from the very beginning – no – I had to stop myself from thinking like that. The way I treated him was all on me, not on him.

He held onto the door as though it was a shield. His body went rigid, tense with fear.

"What do you want?" he asked. His voice trembled with emotion and I could tell he was barely holding himself together.

"I want to talk. I want to explain," I said. That was all I could say for the moment. I wondered what he saw when he looked into my eyes. Did he see someone he could love? Did he see someone that was in pain? Or did he just see a monster?

# Chapter Eleven



I hadn't been expecting anyone to be at my door, certainly not Rudy. When I saw him standing there I was filled with fear. After what we had shared and how he had summarily dismissed me like he was ashamed of me I didn't want to see him. I was afraid of him, and all I wanted was to crawl up into a hole and leave the world behind entirely. There was a lump in my throat that wouldn't go away no matter how many times I tried to swallow, and when I looked at him I honestly didn't know how he was going to react. Was he so tortured that he had come here to torment me again, maybe even beat me down? I'd heard stories about people who were so ashamed of being gay that they used to beat people as a way to punish themselves.

"What's there to explain Rudy? You obviously hate me. You've made that perfectly clear from the first moment we spent together and I've been a fool for ever thinking that something could be different. I think it's time we just end this now. I don't care if you're going to give me a bad recommendation or not. I don't have to put up with this. What you did it's... it's evil," I said, and I couldn't stop my voice from cracking on the words.

"Josh, please."

"No!" I said, surprising myself with the strength of my words. "You don't get to do this again. You don't get to order me around or control me or treat me like shit. I'm a person, damn it! I'm a goddamn person and you don't get to abuse me like this. Just go. Leave me alone. Let all the other people worship you, because I've seen the real you. I know what you are Rudy Marsh. I know what kind of man you are and I've had enough of you."

I went to slam the door in his face because that was the only recourse I had. I wanted him to be out of my life so badly, but he shot out an arm and prevented me from closing the door.

"Josh, you don't know the real me. But I want you to. I want to tell you everything. Please, can I come in?"

I gnawed on my lower lip, wondering if I could trust him. After all he had put me through I didn't think I could, and yet there was a part of me that wanted to give him the benefit of the doubt. Maybe I shouldn't have allowed myself to be so weak, but I was at least going to set up some boundaries.

"We can talk, but not here. I don't want you in my house," I said. I closed the door behind me and we began to stroll along the sidewalk. There was a path that led to a wooded area, and we headed towards this. The moon was bright and the stars twinkled. I dug my hands in my pockets and my gaze kept darting towards him, worried that he was suddenly going to explode with rage. For a few moments we walked in silence. I wondered when he was going to start actually talking to me. Whatever was on his mind must have been heavy, and I waited patiently.

"I'm sorry for the way I've been treating you," Rudy said. I had to check my ears because it was the last thing I expected to hear from him. For all the time we had known each other he had never seemed like someone who would admit when he was wrong, and he never seemed as though he was going to back down from anything. "I know it hasn't been fair to you and you haven't done anything to deserve it. I've been a bastard and I'm sorry. I'm especially sorry for what happened earlier. It was... things got out of hand."

I nodded, still unsure where this was exactly going.

"The truth is," he continued, "that there's only one person in the whole world who knows the real me, and that's Annette. I know you spoke with her, so you probably know that we were together in high school, before I left to start my career. Well, after that I kept myself isolated from other people. I focused on the ice. There's been nothing that's meant anything to me other than the ice, but recently I've started to realize that the ice isn't going to be there forever. Things have been rattling around in my brain, things that I'd rather forget, but I haven't been able to stop them from coming back to me and I think that's why I came back here. I wanted to put certain things to rest, but it hasn't turned out that way at all. It's hard being a public figure. Everyone thinks they know me, but really they just see parts of themselves reflected in me. And I think it's time I started being honest with people, and I figure I might as well start with you."

"Okay," I said, still wary of what Rudy was saying. I noticed that he didn't look at me at all while we were walking together. At one point he stopped to pick up a stone, and then hurled it into the trees. It rustled against the leaves.

"So Annette and I were together in high school. She was sweet and loving and everything anyone could want in a girlfriend, but that wasn't enough for me. There's always been a part of me that's different. I guess I've always known inside, but I tried to fight it because, well, people in small towns like this aren't always the most open minded sort, and there were always a lot of insults thrown around in the locker room. I wanted to project a certain kind of image, so Annette and I were together. And I don't want you to think that I didn't love her, because I did. I still do. But there was someone else. His name was Cody."

I pricked my ears up at this as I hadn't expected this revelation at all. Our pace slowed as we entered the forested area. He leaned against a tree and placed his hand against the bark. I waited patiently for him to speak again. This was a side of Rudy I hadn't seen before, and frankly it was a side that I would never have bet on existing. It was soft and sensitive, and I found that it appealed to me.

"Cody was a guy I played hockey with. He transferred in from the city. His parents got a job out here or something. He was big and fast and a great player. He was the only one who really felt like my equal, and we hit it off straight away. We ran through the leagues and destroyed all the opposition. A lot of teams basically gave up when they saw our names together on the team sheet, and it was great. I'd never had a player who I had such a great connection with. On the ice it felt as though he knew where I was without looking. We just clicked together, and we clicked together off the ice as well.

When I look back now I think I knew from the beginning that there was something special between us, something more than friendship, but at the time it was confusing. I didn't want to be gay and I told myself that we were just good friends. I was with Annette at the time still and I didn't want anything to hurt her. But one night Cody and I were practicing alone together and he came up to me. He told me that there was something on his mind. He got me to lean in because he wanted to whisper it to me, because it was secret, but then he kissed me. It caught me completely by surprise, but I loved it. We dropped our hockey sticks and fell onto the ice, kissing madly, like we'd never kissed before. It was so... electric."

Hearing him talk about this kiss was enlightening, but I had to admit it filled me with envy as well, even though it had occurred years ago.

"We started fooling around more and Annette found out. I hated to hurt her so badly but I explained what was happening in my heart and somehow she found it within herself to forgive me. I'll never understand how anyone could be so kind, and we agreed that we would keep up appearances because I didn't want to get in trouble. But then one day Cody's Dad caught us fooling around and he got mad. I'd never been so scared in all my life. His face was like thunder and I thought he was going to kick my ass. He dragged Cody kicking and screaming back into the house and I never saw him again. They packed up and moved out just like that," he snapped his fingers, "and I never heard from Cody again. For all I know he might as well have dropped off the face of the earth. And since then I guess I just wanted to keep this part of me secret because it feels as though I'm not allowed to have these feelings. I've tried to focus on the ice and on my career, but there are times when I think about Cody and I get so damned angry because it could have been so different. If his Dad had just been a little more understanding…" rage flared in his eyes, but then it settled into deep sorrow.

"So I'm sorry for acting the way I did. I'm not angry at you. I guess I'm angry at the world, and I'm angry at myself for not doing anything differently. In a lot of ways I feel as though I've wasted my life. I haven't let myself fall for anyone again, but then you came along. I think part of the reason why I was so harsh with you was because I didn't want to acknowledge these feelings. I tried to push them away as far as possible, and it led me to treating you like shit. I'm sorry for that."

"And what about what happened today? What was that about?"

"That was me being unable to handle being close to anyone. I've been so afraid that something is going to happen that I've had to stop myself over the years, and it bled out into this. I'm sorry Josh. I hope that this helps explain my actions though."

It certainly did, and I certainly felt bad for him, but there were a few things that I didn't quite understand.

"It sounds horrible what you went through, but this thing with you and me… is there something there or was this just you indulging this part of yourself? I mean, are you actually willing to be open about yourself or are you still going to hold things back?"

"Honestly? I don't know," Rudy said, staring up at the sky. "I just wanted to tell you because these feelings have been tearing me up inside and it's not fair to Annette to keep going to her. She has her own troubles."

"So all this time you've never had anyone to talk to this about? All these years that you've been playing in the major leagues you've never spoken to anyone about this?" I asked.

Rudy shook his head and in that moment he didn't look like that magnificent hockey player that would go down in history as one of the best who had ever skated on the ice. He didn't look like the god among men who was worshiped by so many others. He didn't even look like the bully who had tormented and ridiculed me. Instead he just looked like a man, a hurt and confused man who was lonely. My heart swelled. I walked over to him and took him into my arms. At first I could feel him resist because that's what he had trained himself to do over the course of so many years, but within moments I felt him relax. He was able to fall into my arms and then he wrapped his own arms around me. He shuddered and trembled and then I heard choking sobs slip from his mouth. I held him tightly and made comforting noises, stroking his back and his hair.

The great Rudy Marsh was in my arms, and I had a feeling I was seeing a side of him that nobody else had ever seen before.

*

It took a while for Rudy to calm down enough that he was able to speak without choking on his words.

"I know I've been hard on you, but I've actually admired a lot about you," Rudy said. "You seem to know who you are and what you want out of life."

I smirked. "I'm glad you feel that way, but I can't say it's a true reflection of what I've been feeling. In all honestly you've challenged me and changed me and I've had to do a lot of self reflection about who I am and what I want out of life. I mean, before you I never realized I could feel this way about a man."

"Really? But you were so good at it."

I flashed him a sheepish smile. "I guess it just came naturally to me."

"No, come on, you must have had a boyfriend before," Rudy said.

I shrugged. "Actually I haven't. To be honest I haven't been close with that many people. I always thought there was something wrong with me. I guess I was just confused. Then I spent a lot of time studying and figuring out what to do with my business. I never felt strongly about anyone before and then... and then you came along."

I forced myself to look into his eyes. The intensity of them almost scared me.

"You should hate me for what I did to you," he said quietly.

"I know I should, but I can't. I don't know what it is about you, but I can't bring myself to hate you. There's something going on inside me and I can't stop it. Being with you, being so close to you like that I just... I need it again. I appreciate you telling me why you've been acting like this and what you've struggled with, but you can't keep doing it. I can't take it anymore Rudy. If you're going to stay around here then I need you to be honest with me and listen to me. I need you to trust me."

"That's always been a problem for me, but I think I'm ready," Rudy said. Given all that he had done to me up until this point it might have been naïve of me to believe him, but there was something in the way he looked at me that made me feel as though I could trust him. I finally felt as though I was getting through to the real Rudy, and that was more than I could have hoped for.

I reached out to take his hand, feeling the weight of it in mine, feeling the heat surging through our bodies.

"So are you planning to keep yourself isolated from the world?" I asked. "Are you planning to keep this part of yourself hidden?"

"Not to the people who matter," Rudy said, smiling softly. He leaned in close to me. I could feel the warmth of his breath washing across my face. I closed my eyes and allowed him to kiss me. His lips were soft, his touch tender. The sweetness of his lips was something I had yearned for and I loved the way he kissed me so romantically. A soft moan escaped my mouth and a smile tugged at the corners of my lips. I could feel myself falling for him hard and fast, and what he had said somehow made up for the way he had treated me. He had been my enemy, but now he was my lover, and I knew that it was something I could hold onto tightly, something that I could be proud of. I couldn't deny the feelings that were in my heart and what's more is that I didn't want to. I wanted to be the man who could make Rudy Marsh happy. I wanted to be the one who could heal his heart and make him believe in love again.

I kissed him back with all that I had and then I asked him if he wanted to come back home with me. We walked hand in hand under the moon, cloaked under the darkness. We giggled as we entered my home and I took him to my bedroom. I turned to say something to him, but he wasted no time in gathering me into his arms and embracing me. His lips crashed against mine and his tongue danced with mine. We slipped off each other's clothes, revealing our skin. His was not covered in lotion any longer, but that didn't make it any less impressive. His muscles swelled, his skin was smooth and supple. Just touching it made tingles spread through my body and my heart fluttered.

He smelled fresh, and I wanted to lose myself in his scent. I was ready to accept this part of myself. It felt as though I was embarking on an adventure and he was my guide. Every trace of a finger that ran up my body sent waves of pleasure rippling through me. I loved the way he could thrill me with every touch, and every kiss was like a little piece of heaven. I felt warmer than I ever had before. It was as though a fire had been stoked within me and was beginning to blaze. He pushed me gently and I fell onto the bed, the mattress creaking underneath my weight.

I stared at his glorious form as he pulled down his pants and revealed himself to me. I groaned at the sight of his manhood, something with which I had grown familiar with over the course of the evening. I reached out and touched it and immediately felt complete. Being with him was like living a dream. It was as though he had been plucked from one of my deepest, darkest fantasies and had been made real. There were so many things I wanted to tell him or say to him, but I couldn't find the words, and to be honest my mouth was busy with other things.

I took him into my mouth and sucked him slowly. This time he didn't grab my head and force me to choke on him. He stood there and let me worship him in the only way I knew how. I looked up as I made love to him with my mouth. My jaw still ached from the way he had treated me before, but I battled through the pain for the sake of the pleasure. It didn't take much for it to come flooding through me, making me tremble and tingle and thrum with delight. I could feel my heart soaring and sweat began to seep out of every pore.

Then, to my surprise, Rudy pulled my mouth away. For a moment I wondered if I had done something to upset him, but he wore a sly smile as he descended to his knees. He placed his hands on my thighs and stripped the last item of clothing away. He fondled me and I gasped as I felt his hand running up and down my cock. His grip was tight and he seemed to know just what to do to make me crazy. Shuddering gasps fell from my mouth in a torrent and my entire body felt alive. Then I felt his lips upon me. The sucking sensation was almost enough to make me climax straight away, but somehow I managed to hold on. He was so glorious, so wonderful, and so fucking talented. His hot breath washed over me and the sight of my cock disappearing into his mouth was like manna from heaven. My mind was a whirl and I wasn't sure I was going to cope with this. I thought I was going to faint because the sensations were so overwhelming, so powerful that I felt like I was going to melt.

Rudy was surprisingly gentle with me. He was soft and slow and I arched my head back as he pleasured me.

I think he could feel that I was close to coming because he took his mouth away and smiled. He rose to sit beside me on the bed and we made out a little longer. We fell back and became a mess of limbs, our bodies pressing against each other in a loving and romantic way. My heart swelled and I almost couldn't kiss him enough. It felt as though I couldn't be as close to him as I wanted. I think I would only have been fulfilled if we had actually been able to melt together and blur into one godly being.

But then Rudy looked at me as he placed his fingers in his mouth and then reached down my body. I wasn't sure what he was dong at first, but then it all became clear. He parted my legs and started to rub and caress the most intimate, most sensitive part of me. I closed in on myself and my breath came out in shudders as he stimulated me with his fingers. I nestled against him and he wrapped one arm around me, giving me more intense pleasure than I had ever felt before. I felt vulnerable and scared and exhilarated at the same time, but somehow I knew that Rudy was going to take care of me. He went to kiss me softly, but my mouth was agape and I had somehow lost control of what was happening in my own body. He had control of me. With one touch he could create tremors that quaked through my soul. The world was twisting and tumbling and I was beginning to lose all sense of where I was. Then I felt him move. He pulled my body, turning it over. My back arched as I went on all fours and I felt him move behind me.

I knew what was coming.

I wasn't sure if I was ready for it, but I knew I wanted it.

I braced myself, clutching the sheets of the bed in my trembling fists. My body was primed to be fucked by Rudy and I was just waiting for the blur of pleasure and pain that was going to lance through me like lightning.

# Chapter Twelve

Rudy

Josh was bent over in front of me, all of his flesh on display. It felt good to embrace this part of myself and admit that he was gorgeous. I had known it from the moment I had seen him, but I had been so ashamed of this aspect of myself that I hadn't wanted to admit it. My revulsion for myself had been embodied in the way that I had treated Josh, but now all I wanted was to make love to him and tell him how beautiful he was. I loved the form of his body, how elegant and slender he looked, albeit with some muscle definition as well. To touch his skin was like touching something precious in the world, and I couldn't get enough.

I ran my hands along the curve of his ass and his thighs, bringing him closer to me. I stared at the puckered hole, waiting for me to fill it. He looked so tight and I knew he was going to feel good. I went gentle this time, knowing that he was new to all this. I gasped as I felt us coming together. I felt his body welcoming me, tightening and tensing at the strange sensations. My body seemed to come alive. Primal, natural instincts took hold and I began thrusting back and forth, letting my blood sing with delight. My neck arched back as I felt lightning crackle through me. Letting go of this exhilarating pleasure was more than I had ever wanted.

Josh's moans were music to my ears. I had my hands all over his body, feeling every inch of him. He was burning and sweaty and I couldn't get enough of him. I breathed in the scent of him and it played havoc with my mind. I reached around and felt his hardness, still aroused for me, still waiting for me to have my fun. The bed creaked under our weight and I felt my mind twisted with kaleidoscopic desire. Bright lights seemed to flash all around me and I lost all sense of where I was in the world. It was as though time had lost all of its meaning, as though everything in the world had lost all meaning apart from him.

I groaned and screamed and moaned, but it still didn't feel like it was enough to properly encapsulate the sheer force of pleasure that was writhing inside me. It had been building up for so long and now that it was finally being released I felt free, as though my soul was being liberated from its shackles.

My hand wrapped around Josh's cock, holding it tight, feeling the pleasure thrum through him. I felt so close with him, closer than I had ever felt with Cody. The blazing pleasure pulsed in my mind. It felt like a star was going supernova inside me and I knew it was only a matter of time before it all came crashing through. He was so close. I could feel him tingle. I could hear it in his voice and I wanted to feel him climax. I went hard and deep and let my body take over. I jerked him off with my hand and then it was all coming. I heard his shuddering breath and the way he moaned and tried to stop it, but I wasn't going to let him stop. Come Josh, come, oh fuck, oh god, and there it was, spurting over my hand, flying free. He trembled and the way his body moved sent me over the edge as well. I clung onto his body as the pleasure suddenly hit me like a juggernaut. It was like a bolt of lightning that went right through my body. It crackled and hissed and my eyes clamped shut as I felt it explode.

In that one moment everything was clear. I was free. It was absolutely perfect. My hand was wet and sticky. Josh was curled up, still bracing himself against the pleasure I had given him. The air was thick with lust and I could almost hear a crowd cheering in my mind. I stretched out my arms, feeling triumphant, feeling as though nothing could ever bring me down from this high. Josh had been the missing piece of the puzzle, and I regretted pushing him away for so long.

And then I collapsed to the bed, drained and delirious and breathless.

It was strange really, even though I had been close with Cody all those years ago I felt closer to Josh now. Maybe the added years did something to my state of mind, but as I looked at Josh I felt as though my heart had been unlocked. I had been given a second chance to be honest with myself, and Josh hadn't turned me away. I took his hand and kissed him gently, hoping he knew how much I appreciated this about him.

"I don't think I'm ever going to get tired of this," Josh murmured.

I grinned. "Do you think this counts as training?" I asked.

"It's certainly good cardio," he laughed. "I hope that I can be good for you Rudy. I'm not like the people you know in your world."

"I think that's why I like you so much. I've been trying to pinpoint exactly why I came home after all this time. I think deep down I knew I needed to be here, to have a reminder of my roots and where I came from. I'm not sure that I could share this part of myself with anyone else. I want you to know that I'm going to make it up to you, the way I treated you I mean."

"Rudy you don't-"

"Yes, I do. I've been an ass and that's not who I want to be. I've been holding onto anger and bitterness for too long. It's torn me up inside and I'm not going to let it happen any longer."

"So I can be sure of a good recommendation then," Josh joked.

I smiled at him and nuzzled my face next to his. "The best damn recommendation," I kissed him and then pulled the sheets over us, cuddling up against him. It had been so long since I had felt the simple thrill of being close to someone. I closed my eyes and breathed in Josh's scent. I took joy in the simple fact that he was beside me in bed. It was comforting and soothing, and I realized that it was all I had ever wanted. I wrapped my arms around him and twined my fingers in between his. I whispered in his ear and made him smile, and it felt like absolute perfection. Cuddling with him in this way was almost as satisfying as making love to him was. He touched my heart, and now I felt as though I had an anchor in the world.

*

Josh and I had been working hard to get myself back in good shape before the season started again. The animosity between us had disappeared completely and I wasn't going to treat him as I had before. His grace was unmatched because he could have easily sold our story to the tabloids and get a hefty payday for the sake of my dignity, but instead he reciprocated my feelings and we were inseparable. It was hard to not be as open with each other as we would have liked, but the world could be a cruel place and I wasn't about to subject us to that kind of scrutiny. But there were two people I wanted Josh to meet.

It was a quiet night when I pulled up outside my parent's house. I hadn't spent as much time with them as I perhaps should have, but now that I was with Josh I felt better able to be open with them.

I walked in with Josh. I smiled at Mom and Dad. Mom greeted me with a kiss and Dad shook my hand. They were always so happy to see me. There were times when I wondered why, and I realized that I had bullied my parents almost as much as I had bullied Josh, albeit in a different way. I had taken their pride in me and twisted it into something ugly because I didn't have faith in myself, but I had to accept that they loved me.

And now they were going to have something else to accept about me as well.

"This is Josh, and he's not just my friend. There's something I need to tell you, and it's something that I'm not going to share with the rest of the world. I've been struggling with these feelings for a long time now and part of the reason why I've been so obsessed with hockey is because it has given me something else to focus on. But it's getting to the point now where I have to realize that I have to deal with these feelings. It hasn't always been easy, but Josh has helped me to see that I'm gay. Josh is... Josh is my boyfriend. I know around here people don't like to think about these things and I know you'd have preferred me to end up with Annette but-" I was cut off by my Mom coming to my side.

"Oh Rudy don't be silly. You don't have to apologize for anything. All we've ever wanted is for you to be happy. That's the only thing that has concerned me over the years. I'm just glad you can be this open with us. Oh come in and sit down. You never have to be afraid of being honest with us about anything. We're your parents. We love you," she said, and in that moment I loved her more than anything in the world. They welcomed Josh into my home and they went to get out the old family albums. I have to admit that it was a lovely evening. They took to Josh far quicker than I had, and seeing him with them made me realize how lucky I was to have him in my life. He was patient, compassionate, and loving. He was good for me, and I knew that I was going to have to hold onto him because if I ever took him for granted then he would just go ahead and make someone else happy.

Mom and Dad went through the old photos and it felt good to be appreciated and loved, not by faceless people in the crowd, but by people who knew every facet of me and could love me for who I am. I will always be grateful for my fans and the love they show for me every time I go on the ice, but I'm even more grateful for the love of my family because they're the people who are going to be there for me when I hang up my skates. I'm including Josh and Annette in this as well, and I know that when I finally do retire I'm going to be surrounded by a loving family who only want the best for me.

It feels good to not have to be angry anymore.

It feels good to be happy.

# Epilogue

Josh

Life with Rudy has been a whirlwind. Once we got together we trained hard, and I finally saw what he was truly capable of. He was a determined guy and once he set his mind to something there was nothing that was going to get in his way. He pushed himself to his limits and I was impressed. He managed to work his way back to peak fitness and he broke a few personal bests along the way. He grinned and told me that he felt better than ever, and I could see the weight that had been lifted off his shoulders.

I was just glad that I had managed to play a part in it.

I was a little worried about what was going to happen to us when he returned, but he was one step ahead of me, as he always seemed to be. He asked me if I wanted to go back with him. The offer stunned me, but it wasn't a hard decision to make. He wrote me a damned good recommendation as well. I wasn't ever going to have to worry about getting clients again. With Rudy Marsh's seal of approval, business was going to boom and I could have a life that was better than anything I had ever dreamed of.

*

I was in the stadium. The atmosphere was electric. When Rudy's name was called out the crowd cheered and they gave him a standing ovation. I wondered how many of them realized how fortunate they were to be witnessing him play in the flesh, because he wouldn't be around forever. He was like a monster on the ice. Nobody could keep up with him, and I felt a little bad for Jesus Navarro. The recent signing had been relegated to the bench as Rudy Marsh was relentless. He racked up point after point and there seemed to be no end to his domination.

Jesus Navarro was going to be another one of those who had failed to live up to the challenge that was Rudy Marsh.

Before all this happened I thought I knew Rudy. He was talked about so often that he was a constant presence in my life, but when I actually met him I realized he was a sensitive, vulnerable soul. There was a part of himself that he showed me and only me. There were millions of people all around the world who loved him and worshiped him, but none of them knew him like I did. I felt lucky to be in this position, to be the one who had captured his heart. It wasn't ideal circumstances of course because we couldn't be open, but that was a small price to pay. I was just happy that I could be with him.

All these men were cheering for a man I loved and I swelled with pride.

Someone came up to stand beside me. "I've seen you around, you're Rudy's personal trainer, right?" he asked.

I smiled to myself and nodded.

"Yeah, that's right," I replied, but deep inside I knew I was so much more than that. I was Rudy Marsh's lover, and that meant the world to me.

*****

# Don't miss out!

Visit the website below and you can sign up to receive emails whenever Van Cole publishes a new book. There's no charge and no obligation.

https://books2read.com/r/B-A-RTRV-TXKDC

# Also by Van Cole

3 Man Huddle: MMM Best Friend Romance
His Alpha Wolf: Gay First Time Romance
A Dragon's Miracle: Gay Dragon MPREG Romance
Double-Teamed: MMM First Time Football Romance
His Football Star: Gay Second Chance Romance
Love In My Town: MM First Time Romance
Training A Hockey Star
Game Night
Double Shift
Take A Shot
Dear Professor
Getting Inked
Ninth Inning
Triple Threat
Seducing My Best Friend's Brother
My Protector
The Blueprint
Show Me The Way
End Zone
Matched To His Tiger
Love At First Puck
My Straight Boss
Falling For The Alpha
My Boss
On Thin Ice

9 7 9 8 2 2 3 3 3 5 7 8 8